MORGAN'S WAR

Mike Morgan wanted his railroad company to be the first to lay track from the Mexican coast to the mines of Matarote. But his rival had other ideas: Mike's workers were murdered, his tunnel destroyed and a locomotive blown up. And when he fell for his financier's daughter Rosa, her father Don Emilio Terrazos was not pleased. Morgan had to take on the hired killers — but against such odds, could he save his railroad and win back Rosa?

HENRY REMINGTON

MORGAN'S
WAR

Complete and Unabridged

LINFORD
Leicester

First published in Great Britain in 2007 by
Robert Hale Limited
London

First Linford Edition
published 2008
by arrangement with
Robert Hale Limited
London

British Library CIP Data

Remington, Henry
    Morgan's war.—Large print ed.—
Linford western library
    1. Western stories
    2. Large type books
    I. Title
    823.9'2 [F]

    ISBN 978–1–84782–397–7

Published by
F. A. Thorpe (Publishing)
Anstey, Leicestershire

Set by Words & Graphics Ltd.
Anstey, Leicestershire
Printed and bound in Great Britain by
T. J. International Ltd., Padstow, Cornwall

This book is printed on acid-free paper

1

'Stand by for blasting. Everybody back outa the tunnel!'

Mike Morgan bellowed the words as he prepared to hit the plunger to dynamite through solid rock. 'Fire ho!'

He was the last to back off as the explosion roared and almost rocked him off his boots. Dust billowed from the tunnel entry as he emerged and grinned at the *peons*.

'OK, boys, git back in there and set to shovelling.'

The tall Texan shook his tousled hair from his eyes, wiped sweat and dirt from his face and glanced back down the valley through the labyrinthine ravines as he heard the gasping huff, huff, huffing of the steam-engine. It was labouring up the steep and winding track they had laid, first from the west sea coast to the plateau, and on up from the town of Santa Rosa.

Steam pirouetted into the thin air of the Sierra Madre, which rose before them to a snow-clad volcanic peak more than 12,000 feet high.

Morgan frowned as the sturdy locomotive gradually climbed closer, for it sounded from the clanging and clattering on the rails as if its trucks were mostly empty.

'Where 'n hell's the cement and iron props we ordered?' he shouted at his elderly partner, Pop Clancy. 'This don't sound good.'

When the big engine hauled in among the tents and scattered equipment of the railroad camp Morgan's fears proved right for all it was carrying was basic supplies: tools, iron rails, sleepers and ties.

The greasy-faced driver in his goggles leaned from the cab and offered an envelope to the bald-headed Clancy, who tore it open and squinted at a handwritten letter. 'It's from Don Emilio — '

'Waal, what does he say?' Morgan demanded, impatiently.

'Your specifications do not call for a cement lining to the tunnel . . . far too costly . . . that's about the gist of it.' Pop made a wry face and passed the letter across. 'Getting dough outa that haughty *haciendado* ain't easy, *amigo*. I told ya we shoulda gone around this damn mountain and built a bridge across the ravine.'

'Yeah, and how much more would that have cost?' Morgan tried to decipher the Spanish lingo of the letter. Don Emilio's quill-pen scrawl didn't help. 'If we don't get that lining up, one of these days . . . '

It was as if the Lord on high had heard his words for suddenly an ominous rumble reverberated from the tunnel. There were shouts and screams as more dust poured from its mouth. One of these days had arrived.

'There's been a fall!' Morgan stated the obvious as he jammed his Stetson back on his head and ran back into the dark hole. Injured workers were groping their way out, mostly walking wounded, but one with a bloody leg obviously broken, needing support. Their foreman, Rowdy Newman, appeared holding a lantern aloft. 'There's two men trapped under them rocks, or else on t'other side,' he drawled. 'Personally, I wouldn't bet on gettin' 'em out alive. That's the worst fall yet.'

'We'll get 'em out,' Mike Morgan roared. 'Get every spare hand digging. You give up too easy, pal.'

'I face the facts,' the curly-bearded Texan muttered more to himself. 'This ain't the hard rock we thought it was. It's unstable. We cain't go on like this. The tunnel needs shoring up.'

Pop shook his head, a worried look on his face. 'Try telling that to Don Emilio.'

'Aw, it's all very well for him, sat in his fancy town house back in Santa Rosa.' Rowdy spat out dust. 'Come on, Pop, let's git these guys organized in a rescue team. Looks to me like they're jest about ready to mutiny. Better set 'em diggin' 'fore they do.'

Three hours later the exhausted team came from the tunnel stretchering an injured man. But the arms of a second *peon* hung lifeless as he was carried. Another sudden cave-in over their heads hadn't helped matters, making the rescuers scatter in fear for their own lives.

Nobody knew much about the corpse, who he was or where he came from, except that his name was Pedro. Just an itinerant worker from the south. In some ways that was a relief to Morgan. He wouldn't have to bear the news to the man's family, not the most pleasant of jobs.

'We'll bury him here,' he said, hurling his spade into a patch of ground. 'Let's git him planted and tamped down.' He looked up at a condor, with its huge wingspan, wheeling on the warm air currents high above. 'Better pile some rocks on top, boys. That varmint thinks he's spotted his supper.'

Morgan felt it was incumbent on him to say a few words and he racked his memory for consolation from the Good Book. He removed his hat and began: 'Pedro was hardworking and loyal. He would have toiled on to see this project through, like I hope y'all will. We bid his soul all speed unto the heavenly kingdom.'

The only phrase he could think of to add was, 'The last shall be first and first last, for many may be called but few chosen.'

'Good luck to him,' Rowdy chuckled. 'There sure ain't much chance of the last coming first here in Meh-hee-co.'

'You boys have been promised a three-day weekend leave for the fiesta of San Geronimo,' Morgan announced, knowing he couldn't stop the *peons* taking leave of absence, anyway. 'So, men, let's put the injured in the caboose and head back down to Santa Rosa. OK?'

'Right!' Pop Clancy might be short and scrawny but he had a peppery temper. 'You can draw half your pay now. You won't get the rest 'less you report back for duty on Tuesday. In the meantime we'll try to sort out some way of improving safety.'

Rowdy gave a rebel whoop and punched the air. 'Count me in, Pop. Let's git red-eyed an' rowdy fer three glorious days. Amen. Allelujah!'

★   ★   ★

They had been buddies from way back, Mike Morgan and Rowdy, starting without a bean, catching the last of the cattle boom, herding beeves on the long, hard trail north from San Antone, crossing Indian Territory to the cow-towns of Kansas, boozing, carousing and brawling in bars from Abilene to Dodge. In 1890 came the big run when the Indian Nations were opened for settlement, 50,000 racing to stake a claim in a land soon to be named Oklahoma.

Mike had hankered to better himself,

7

but saw little profit in either prodding beeves or ploughing the land. Oil was said to be the next big thing and he had tried wildcatting, but made little cash from the black gold. Bull-riding seemed a better way to make a fast buck. But it was a matter of 'easy come, easy go' when he and Rowdy hit the rodeo circuit.

They were in a bar in Oklahoma City when they bumped into Pop Clancy. He might be college-educated, a trained engineer and surveyor, but he was hitting the liquor hard. Apparently his wife had run off with a younger man and he was on the skids.

'It ain't no use looking at life through the wrong end of a bottle,' Morgan had advised him. 'You gotta pull yourself outa it, pal.'

'Aw, all I need is a stake and I'd go back to building railroads,' the older man told him. 'That's where the the cash is.'

Already a network of lines criss-crossed the Territory. Pop had worked for the big Kansas & Texas Company. His dream was to go it alone, have his own outfit, get a share of the profits. 'They're crying out for engineers in southern Texas and Mexico,' he said. 'We could start our own company.'

Mike was celebrating winning Horseman of the Year rodeo title and it so happened he was flush with $5,000 prize money in his pocket. 'Sure am tired of being bounced off bulls,' he drawled. 'How about if I invested my cash in you, would that be enough to set us up?'

'It would be a start!' Pop had stuck out his hand. 'Put it there, kid. I'm gonna teach you everything I know about building railroads. And more.'

It was a big gamble, but so far it had paid off. Fired by the younger man's enthusiasm Pop had straightened out and their partnership had prospered. Mike might be unschooled, but he was quick witted and eager to learn. Southern Texas and Arizona had been opened up by their railroads.

When they heard that a wealthy Mexican landowner was looking for a railroad company to extend the line from Puerto on the coast to Santa Rosa, up through the mountains to the tin-mines of Matarote and was willing to put big money into the venture, it had seemed like a golden opportunity.

But as they chugged on down in the empty trucks to Santa Rosa, Morgan reflected that this job was not going to be as easy as it had first looked. In Texas it had been a simple matter of laying beds and rails in straight lines across the rolling flat-lands from one objective to another. These great ravines and canyons they were crossing were a different kettle of fish.

The mountains rose like a steep wall from a fertile plateau, most of it, as far as the eye could see, owned by Don Emilio Terrazos. Through this domain ran a sparkling river bordered by lush fields, with maize, olives, vines, peach-orchards, and vegetable crops where his peons toiled. Beyond were more rugged

10

lands where *vaqueros* tended his bulls and cattle. This might be the late nineteenth century but the don still lived in almost feudal splendour.

However, Don Emilio realized that the days of transporting goods by mule train and cart were long over. Tin, like copper and lead, was almost as precious as silver. There was a worldwide market. What was needed was a railroad to transport it from the mines to the main line and coastal ports. And their job was to provide him with that railroad.

When they came clanging and clanking into the small colonial-style town of Santa Rosa, they saw to the needs of the injured men, then headed for the nearest cantina to cut the dust from their throats.

'I'm gonna tell Señor Terrazos that it ain' no use him tryin' to cut costs on an operation like this,' Mike growled, as he sank a tankard of beer. 'One man's dead. We don't want no more fatalities.'

'You leave this to me,' Pop said. 'I'm gonna go visit the barber shop and git spruced up 'fore we meet. I don't want you going barging in there shaking your horns at him.'

'I believe in plain speaking. We gotta tell him we need a lining for that tunnel. Once we're through it'll be an easy climb.'

'You gotta remember Don Emilio's the money-man, Mike. We don't want him getting upset and pulling the plug on us. We gotta use a little diplomacy, win him round to our way of thinking.'

'Aw, OK, you go see him. Me an' Rowdy'll wait an' see how you get on. But don't let that coyote wriggle outa his responsibilities. Meanwhile we'll take a little rest and relaxation with the boys.'

'OK, Mike, you do that.' Pop slapped his shoulder. 'But don't go paintin' the town red like last time. I don't want to have to bail you outa the gendarmerie.'

'Aw, jest 'cause you've signed the pledge,' Rowdy yelled after him as he departed, 'you jest don't like to see us having fun. You ornery ol' buzzard.'

2

'What's this?' Don Emilio held his steak suspended 'twixt knife and fork. 'Did I call for the cobbler to mend my boots?'

The cook, dragged from the kitchen of the grandly named Hotel Real in his greasy apron, hung his head as he stood before them. 'No, your excellency.'

'So, are you hard of hearing?' The *haciendado* raised his voice as he tossed the meat back at the man, contemptuously. 'I asked for medium rare, not frizzled to death, you dolt. Take it. Get out of my sight.'

Pop Clancy sat stony-faced through their host's tantrum, fingering the uncomfortable stud of his celluloid collar which he had donned for the occasion with his best — well, only — linen suit. This querulous don sure was a fastidious little creep. The seven-course dinner was going on for

13

an age. Starting with olives and smoked sausages, egg soup, a bony trout, pâté with sauce, and now the offending main course with its side-salads, there were still pudding and cheeses to negotiate before they could settle down and talk business.

Don Emilio, with his coiffed, greying hair, in his traditional black velveteen, pearl-decorated suit, smiled in his conceited manner at his fellow guests. 'I am paying for my own beef I sold them. You would think they might attempt to grill it as instructed.'

Two upper-crust gents and their ladies at the table grinned gaily, undisturbed. They were used to Don Emilio's whims. He was one of the richest landowners in the state, so he was entitled to pick and choose.

'These peasants, they are such a trial,' one of the women remarked.

Only Don Emilio's daughter, Rosa, seemed unamused. A girl of nineteen years, she was dressed like the others in the height of Mexican fashion in rustling Spanish lace and flame-coloured satin, her shiny black hair piled high on her head and held by an amber comb. There were pearls around her pale, slim neck and diamonds on her wrist and at her ears. She had inherited her father's haughty mien, but was, of course, softer, more feminine. Pop thought she had sad, dark eyes, the air of a caged songbird.

Suddenly, she was speaking to Pop. 'I understand you lost a man killed in a fall. I was wondering, was he local? We ought to do something for his family.'

'Pah, what does it matter?' her father exclaimed, sipping at his wine. 'He was just another *peon*.'

'You make it sound as if he might be some dog,' Rosa protested. 'He was a human being, Papa.'

'Rosa has suddenly developed a social conscience.' Don Emilio laughed. 'Perhaps I should put her in a convent.'

'She has an interesting point,' one of the overfed men grunted. '*Peons*, Indians, the lowest of the low. Often I wonder, *can* they be human? *Do* they possess souls?'

'We couldn't find out much about Pedro,' Pop butted in through the laughter. 'He was from somewhere down south. We gave him a Christian burial. That's all we could do. There's gonna be more deaths unless something's done. Your father knows the answer.'

'Sir!' Don Emilio retorted. 'This is not a fit conversation for the dining-table. We will discuss it in private later over brandy and cigars.'

Pop shrugged and went to attacking his steak. 'This tastes fine to me,' he muttered, 'after the grub we been getting in the camp the last five weeks.'

* * *

'Hey, *muchacha*!' Rowdy gave a yell as he wound his arm around a buxom Indian woman as they sported, naked as nature intended, in a huge wooden barrel of suds. 'That ain't the soap you

16

got your hands on!'

Mike Morgan towelled his curly hair as he sprawled half-dressed at a table and chair in the bodega-cum-brothel beneath a row of barrels containing sherry and wine. 'That was good,' he said to the dark girl beside him. She was skinny to the point of scarecrow bony, but he didn't like too much weight on a woman. 'How much I owe ya?'

'Please, you geev ten pesos,' she pleaded, opening her palm to him. 'I have baby to feed.'

'Yeah? You don't say? Here.' He tossed twenty to her. 'Keep the change.' She didn't look like the usual harlot. Too shy and tentative. Maybe she was just a beginner. 'Say, why don't you put your fine feathers on and come out and show us the town?'

'I don't know whether I should,' she demurred in Spanish.

'I'll pay ya extra for your time and fix it with the boss man.' He flicked ten more silver pesos across. 'Come on. It's jest that I hanker for some female company. Ain't had none in an age. We'll have some fun.'

Rowdy had clambered from the tub, opened the bung of one of the barrels and, head back, was catching a stream of liquor in his mouth, or trying to.

'Don't git paralytic jest yet. I ain't carryin' you back to the hotel. Git your drawers on,' Mike yelled. 'We're goin' dancing. The gals are coming along.'

They staggered out of the brothel and weaved their way arm-in-arm along the narrow cobbled street that wound through the high-balconied houses. Rowdy spotted a glow of candlelight and dragged them diving down steps and through the bead-hung doorway of a small *pulqueria*. He grinned at the barman and its morose occupants and yelled, 'Time for tequila. Set up the ammunition, mister. We're celebrating.'

'What we got to celebrate?' Mike asked as he knocked back a shot.

'Dunno,' Rowdy smirked, stroking his bushy beard, 'but there must be somethang. Oh, yeah, it's fiesta.'

'Not until tomorrow.'

'Aw, well, we're starting early.'

★　★　★

'Our great benefactor, President Porfirio Diaz, welcomes Americanos to our country if they can help us modernize Mexico and improve trade.' Don Emilio nodded at a portrait of the grim, moustachioed dictator on the hotel wall. 'So I will do all in my power to ensure the success of our project. Within reason, of course.'

Pop Clancy had at last got him to talk business as they sat in a corner of the hotel foyer. 'We gotta have a lining to the tunnel. Every time we set dynamite we bring down a section of the roof on our heads.'

'As I said in my note there is no specification for this in the contract. Cement is expensive. You are asking for more money. My money. I will make my own decision on this.'

'We've sunk a lot of our own company's cash in this, too,' Pop protested. 'We've provided our own rolling-stock, the two locomotives, the trucks, the tools and equipment, the expertise. You can't start cutting costs now.'

'I can do as I wish,' Don Emilio snapped.

His daughter and friends were sitting apart, joined by a young Mexican in a dark suit. 'This is my protégé,' Don Emilio said, beckoning him across. 'You may be interested in his news.'

Ferdinand Lopez was tall and muscularly built for a Mexican. He was handsome in his way, his long black hair greased back, but there was a brutal jut to his jaw. He also wafted of strong, sickly perfume. He spoke with an American twang in a deep husky voice. 'You ain't the only one interested in laying a track to Matarote, buddy.'

'What do ya mean?' Pop asked, genuinely stunned.

'Some Californian company is making a survey right now. They're talking of going along the river and cuttin' up to the mines across the side of the volcano.'

'But that's crazy.' Pop was trying to come to terms with this awesome news. 'They would need to lay another sixty miles of track.'

'With their funds I doubt whether that would bother them.' Lopez showed his white teeth in a sharklike grin. 'It's hefty competition, Mr Clancy. There's a lot at stake here. They've smelt the chance of making fat money.'

'They can't do that. It ain't right. We were here first.' Pop was flustered, a sense of panic rising in his gorge. 'How do you know this? You been havin' talks with 'em?'

Don Emilio smiled. 'Ferdinand keeps his ear to the ground.'

'Are you saying you're thinking of going in with 'em? You cain't do this. You signed a contract.'

'It was more of a gentleman's agreement which I will abide by. But I am a businessman. If this other company proves it can get to Matarote before you, well . . . ' he shrugged, 'I may be forced to reconsider our deal. So, I suggest you get back on the job. If you can't go through the mountain, go around it. Build bridges. There is plenty of timber up there you can use.'

'It's not just timber,' Pop protested. 'We will need cement for the bridges' foundations, more men.'

'Out of the question, if I'm footing the wages bill. It is high enough already. You will have to do what you can with what you have.' Don Emilio waved his hand as if the matter was dismissed and turned to his protégé. 'Well, Ferdinand, will you be escorting Rosa to the ball tomorrow night?'

'With your permission, sir, I would be honoured.'

'Good. Shall we rejoin my guests?'

★ ★ ★

'He's as drunk as a skunk,' Mike said, as Rowdy was supported along the street by the huge whore, her bosom trembling with mirth as she tried to hang onto him. 'He jest cain't take the tequila. We'd better git him back to the hotel.'

They had bumped into Pat Murphy, the gang boss, in a bar, wielding as always his shillelagh, the knobbly club with which he urged their *peons* on to greater endeavours, and a couple of his Irish *compadres*. Suddenly they heard the clatter of horses' hoofs coming up the cobbled lane behind them, and they scattered as two riders charged past. 'Get outa the damn way,' one shouted.

'Americans. Where they come from?' Morgan wondered as he hugged the skinny Teresa into him.

The two men wore range clothes, slouch hats and bandannas, with carbines jutting from the saddle boots of their powerful beasts. Mud-splattered, they looked as though they had come a long distance. 'What are they doing here?' Morgan wondered again.

When they reached the Hotel Real he found the riders' horses tethered outside. While it might not be as regal as its name implied for this outback of Mexico the establishment was regarded as top grade. At least the beds were bug free. It was a bit above the likes of Murphy and company, who were boarded elsewhere. But, in his elated state, Mike shouted, 'Come on in, boys, I'll buy y'all a night-cap.' He had never paid much heed to society's caste system. Nor did it occur to him, for that matter, that the two rouged and skimpily clad whores might not be welcome.

So they all barged noisily into the hotel foyer and across to the bar, shouting for service. The two *hombres*, unshaven, in their ratty riding-coats and wide-brimmed hats, stood at one end and eyed them malevolently.

'Howdy,' Rowdy greeted them, sticking out a paw. 'Guess you boys must be from the good ol' land of the free. What brings you bozos into Santa Rosa? Here fer the fiesta?'

The nearer one regarded him coldly

and ignored his hand. 'What the hell's that to you?'

His tubby companion spat a gob at an overfull spittoon in a corner, missed, and grinned over broken teeth. 'Bozos he called us, Hank. You gonna take that from him?'

Rowdy swayed as the overweight Indian woman held him upright. 'Only tryin' to be amiable to fella Amer'cuns, friend,' he sang out in his sawtooth drawl. 'What makes you two so high and mighty?'

'Let me take a guess.' The one named Hank struck a match on his thumb and lit a cheroot. 'A pig-faced runt like you must be connected to this half-assed railroad bunch we been hearin' about. Me an' Lefty have come up here to see just what you're up to.'

'What?' Rowdy drunkenly drew back his fist as if to strike a blow. 'What did you call me?'

Morgan caught hold of his arm to restrain him. 'OK. Calm down. You ain't in no fit state. Ignore 'em.'

He didn't care for the looks or attitude of these two. Nor for the glimpse of the shooting-irons they were packing beneath their coats. He had seen their like swaggering in saloons of the Oklahoma panhandle, known as No Man's Land, haunt of outlaws and criminals on the lam. He gently pressed Rowdy to one side and met their hard, hat-shadowed eyes.

'No offence, friends,' he said, 'but just what would your interest be in the railroad we're building?'

The short one, Lefty, grinned tauntingly. '*Tryin*' to build, ya mean, doncha?'

'What you gettin' at?' Morgan was trying to remain calm but, tequila-fuelled, he felt his rage rising. 'Why doncha spit it out?'

'OK. We will do.' The tall one, in his spur-jangling, high-heeled boots stood a similar strapping six-foot-two to Mike Morgan and he eyed him evenly, as cigar smoke trickled from his thin lips. 'It's like this. Your operation's over.

Kaput. All wrapped up. Geddit? Our boys are moving in. You better get that into your thick skull. You an' your bogtrotter pals can hightail it pronto back to Texas, or wherever they come from. Or thangs could git nasty.'

Murphy and his two pals were busy claiming their free drinks, but Murphy cocked his head at this, roaring like a bull, 'What was dat he called us?'

'Bogtrotters.' The shorter *hombre* grinned. 'You heard, half-wit. The sooner you're outa Mexico the healthier it'll be for you.'

'Hang on,' Morgan said. 'Do I take it you two are working for the K and T?'

'You can take it how the hell you like,' the tall one replied. 'That's for you to guess and us to know.'

'You lousy sidewinders.' Rowdy hurled himself forward and swung a haymaker. Unluckily, his alcoholic state didn't improve his aim. The tall man, Hank, grabbed his flailing arm and sent him spinning to land on his backside in the spittoon.

'Friggin' hail,' Rowdy moaned as he

27

sat amid the slime, and a bottle swung by Lefty clonked on his cranium.

Tequila hadn't improved Morgan's aim much, either. His right fist rocketed out but only brushed the stubble of Pike's jaw. Pike's gloved fist thudded into his ribs and made him gasp. Pike's knee jerking up into his crotch didn't help.

Suddenly bedlam broke out in the bar as Murphy and his beefy Irish boyos rushed into the scrum. The runty desperado screamed shrilly as a flailing shillelagh cracked across his elbow, then back, against his knees. Furniture crashed, glasses smashed, as he was bodily picked up and hurled across the counter. The girls screamed hysterically, getting in the way as Pike and Morgan wrestled and swapped blows.

Across the foyer in their armchairs Don Emilio, his daughter and guests, peered through the potted palms. 'My God!' the *haciendado* cried. 'What's going on?'

He beckoned furiously to the hotel

manager. 'How dare you allow those scum in here? Go summon the *rurales*, immediately.'

The bald-headed manager stared at him, pop-eyed, like a rabbit before a stoat. 'It is the *Americanos*, excellency.'

'The *Americanos*! I might have known.' Don Emilio jumped to his feet, pointing a finger. 'Is that your partner?' he demanded of Clancy. 'Disgraceful!'

'Yeah,' Pop groaned. 'It looks like it is.'

Suddenly Pike's fist had hammered into Morgan's chest and, caught unbalanced, Morgan came back-pedalling from the scrum to land in a heap at the feet of Don Emilio and his guests. He looked up, met Rosa's startled, dark eyes and Don Emilio's disapproving ones. 'Excuse me, folks.' He struggled onto his feet and started, unsteadily, back into the fight. He stopped short when he found himself looking down the barrel of Pike's Colt. 'Whoa,' he muttered. 'Hold it boys.'

'Yeah, you better,' Pike snarled.

His *compadre* came up from behind the bar, a gun in his hand covering them, too. For seconds Morgan was unsure whether or not they would shoot. It was a life or death moment. 'Don't be stupid,' he gasped. 'We ain't armed.'

'Lucky for you,' Hank Pike said, swinging the revolver threateningly at the Irish, making them back off. 'C'mon, Lefty. These hogs have had enough. Let's git outa here.'

He picked up his hat, jammed it down over his brow, went to the bar, took his glass with his spare hand, calmly downed its contents, and strode out, followed by Lefty. At the door he turned to them, the revolver trained on Morgan. 'Be warned. Next time you won't get away scot free. Take my advice. Get outa this country. While you're still alive.'

3

'Them sorta guys fight dirty,' Rowdy Newman complained as he fingered the sticky wound caused by the bottle-blow to the back of his head. 'I'd kinda forgotten that.'

'Dose *rurales* weren't partic'lar where dey poked deir bayonets, either,' the burly Murphy muttered as he tenderly rubbed his posterior. 'I won't be able to sit down for days.'

When the guardians of the president's pyramid of power, five uniformed *rurales* stationed in the town, had arrived in the hotel, Don Emilio had pointed to the miscreants, and the five lawmen had laid about them with gusto. By that time the two desperadoes, Pike and Lefty, had climbed on their horses and were well away. With blows and curses the American railroad men were arrested and herded along to the hoosegow.

The cell in which they were now sprawled was an adobe construction with barred windows through which drifted sounds of jollity: firecrackers exploding, guitars strumming, bells ringing, laughter and screams of excitement as the populace celebrated San Geronimo's day. 'Sounds like dey are havin' a right hooley,' one of the Irish remarked as he helped himself to a drink of stagnant water from a barrel, the only sustenance provided.

There were no bunks so they had to lie on the floor or stand around. 'Yeah,' Mike Morgan growled. 'I'm gittin' too old for this kinda caper. I'm s'posed to have reached the age of responsibility, or so Pop told me. Wish I'd listened to him.'

'Where is he?' Rowdy wondered. 'We been in here all day. Why ain't he come to our rescue?'

'What bothers me,' Mike muttered, 'is that while we've been stuck in here them two coyotes could be causin' all kinda mayhem.'

'They've probably gawn back to report to their bosses,' Rowdy said. 'They'll be nursin' their bruises same as us.'

'Maybe.' What bothered Morgan was the ominous significance of the two riders' appearance in Santa Rosa. If it was true that another organization was trying to muscle in on their operation it did not bode well. He knew Pop had rustled up all the capital available, taken a gamble on this enterprise, dreaming of big profits. If the rug was pulled from under them now that would be the end of the dream.

All day Rowdy had been hollering and demanding attention. But there had not been a tremor of interest in their plight. It was as if they were forgotten and entombed. Then, suddenly, a big oak door along the end of the passage was unlocked. It creaked open and a *rurale*, in scarlet cape and sombrero stomped towards them, followed by Pop Clancy.

'Waal, talk of the devil,' Rowdy

whooped. 'Ye've sure taken your time.'

'I couldn't help it, boys. They wouldn't let me in,' Pop whined. 'It's your own fault. You've let us down, badly, all of you. They say you insulted the president. Who threw the bottle that ruined the portrait of the ol' buzzard? If you were *peons* you'd be hanged. As it is they're talkin' about deportation.'

'What?' Rowdy screeched. 'Have you told 'em they've got the wrong guys. It was them other two — '

'All right,' Pop said. 'I paid all the damages, and sweeteners to those jokers. They've dropped the charges. It's cost me a pretty penny. I'm gonna have to stop it outa your wages. Don't argue. Let's git you outa here.'

★ ★ ★

The Chinese cook, Wang the Fang, as they called him due to his one solitary tooth, had been left to look after the camp while the boys were away. It was lonesome in the mountains all on his own. When he spotted two strangers, in long riding-coats and wide-brimmed hats urging their mustangs at a fast clip up the track towards him he experienced a sense of apprehension. He said a prayer to his ancestors for protection as they approached.

'You the only one around?' Hank queried as they reined in.

'Yah, mister. Boss and boys gone.'

'Just one Chink in charge,' Lefty drawled, as he whirled his horse around and noticed a large steel bin with a skull and crossbones painted on the front. 'That's a mite careless of 'em, ain't it?'

'How far they got with the tunnel?' Hank demanded, peering up the track to the dark hole in the hillside.

'Oh, 'bout quarter-mile. But no good. Bad trouble. Man dead. They gone. You go look,' Wang sang out, 'if you wan'.'

'We will,' Lefty remarked, as he swung down. 'This where they keep the explosives, is it?'

'No.' Wang waggled a forefinger at

him. 'You no touch.'

Lefty brought out his revolver and swiped the cook across the jaw. Wang dropped, pole-axed. 'Me no touchee,' Lefty crowed, and shot through the padlock of the bin. 'Waal, whadda ya know?' he called. 'This should do nicely.'

'Yeah!' Hank Pike gave his crooked grin. 'Trouble? They don't know the meaning of the word.'

When the Chinaman moaned Lefty bludgeoned him again. He slung him across the back of Hank's horse, gathered an armful of explosives, detonators and a coil of fuse wire, and led the way into the tunnel. When they reached the recent fall they dumped Wang among the rubble and set about wiring the whole tunnel. Lefty returned to the bin and came rattling back with a barrow loaded with more dynamite. 'This is gonna make one helluva bang,' he cackled.

'Come on, let's git outa here!' Hank shouted, when he had set the last detonator and uncoiled the wire back down the track. He pressed down the plunger and paused to hear the rumble and roar as the whole mountain shook. Rocks and dust burst forth, raining through the air as the dynamite went off. Hank Pike felt the blast on his back as he ran to scramble on to his mustang and hared away after his sidekick.

'That'll give 'em something to chaw on.' Lefty chuckled as they reined in and turned to watch a huge dust cloud rolling upwards into the blue sky.

★　★　★

Mike Morgan felt more human after he had had a good sleep at the hotel, bathed and shaved and put on clean pants and a new white shirt. 'It ain't no use going back to the camp,' he said as he sipped a glass of rusty-tasting beer, cooled with ice brought from the mountains, on the veranda of the Real. 'The *peons* won't come with us 'til this religious shindig is over.'

'I don't mind admitting I'm worried,' Pop muttered. 'Crossed my mind to head down to Puerto, see if I can locate whoever's running this rival company. If they're employing thugs like them two we may be in trouble.'

'Ain't these *rurales* stationed here meant to protect us?'

'They're recruited from the scum of the prisons to keep the *peons* under the heel. Unless they get direct orders from above they'll only protect them who pays 'em best. They've got a different system in this country. The *mordida*, the bribe, is everything.'

'Waal,' Mike drawled, 'in that case I'd better dig my ol' S an' W outa my trunk. Maybe we should think about arming the men, too.'

'Hold your hosses, son. We ain't lookin' for real trouble. Let's see what develops.' Pop stirred his coffee and watched the Sunday morning parade of townspeople who were heading towards the big mission church that towered above the rooftops. 'Anyhow, them two coyotes ain't broke the law yet. According to Don Emilio it was you boys who started the ruckus.'

'Huh! Ain't he s'posed to back us up?'

Morgan knocked back the beer and considered their situation. He was worried. He had an uneasy feeling that all was not right up at the camp. 'Tell you what I'm gonna do, old pal — I'm gonna buy me a half-decent horse along at the corral so I can scout around. I'll see ya back at the tunnel.'

'Don't do anything foolish, Mike. Try to control that temper of yourn,' Pop advised. 'You know, I ain't gittin' any younger. I was hoping I might be able to retire on my share of the proceeds from this one. It had occurred to me to put down roots and just run this track to and from the mines in partnership with Don Emilio. But somehow I feel it all slipping through our fingers.'

'Not without a fight, old-timer. We're gonna be the first to the tin-mines. I can assure you of that.'

'I can only hope so.'

Morgan tugged his Stetson rakishly down over his brow to shield his eyes from the harsh morning sunlight. 'Hey,' he drawled, brightening up. 'Ain't that Don Emilio's daughter?'

An open landau drawn by two dappled greys had been forced to a halt by the throng right outside the hotel. Two females in church-black dresses, a girl with a mantilla draped around her head, and an older woman, possibly her mother, were seated in the back. Morgan met Rosa's mischievous eyes as she glanced up at him, and he raised fingers to his hat-brim in salute. For seconds their eyes locked and it was as if they were the only two people who counted in all that throng.

The coachman found a space, flicked his whip and the carriage moved on its way towards the church doors. 'Wow!' Mike exclaimed. 'What a beaut!'

'Hold it, buster. You keep your eyes offen her,' Pop ordered. 'She's Don Emilio's only daughter. Her mother died in childbirth. She's been pampered and cosseted all her life. She has a life-style you couldn't afford. Don Emilio told me he would only countenance a man of noble birth, and, no doubt, with plenty of moolah, as her suitor. Forget that baby, Mike. She's not for you.'

'Maybe, maybe not.' Morgan was getting to his feet and he grinned at the older man. 'It's fiesta time, Pop. What's the harm in a little flirtation?'

'Don't do it, Mike, please,' the older man begged. 'Leave her alone. Or you'll really upset the apple-cart.'

'Aw, you worry too much, old-timer. It's time I went to say my prayers.'

Pop watched Morgan go striding away towards the church and sighed. Rodeo riders had quite a reputation among the ladies and Mike was no exception. 'Yeah, sure,' he tried to convince himself. 'He's got no chance. He'll never git past that duenna. She guards her night and day, fierce as a mastiff.'

★ ★ ★

The interior of the church was more like a cathedral. There was a plethora of ornamentation in gold and silver around the high altar, the massed congregation shuffled and whispered, a choirboy swung a censer and incense wafted its dry perfume. There were no chairs, so most of the *peons* either stood or knelt on the bare flagstones. However, around the walls were private shrines and pews set aside for the landowners or wealthy trades people. Scanning them, Mike saw that Rosa and her duenna were seated in one up near the altar, so he made his way forward. An old priest, in his exotic robes, had climbed to a pulpit high above their heads, and, like an intercessor with God, was singing out his Latin. It was all mumbo-jumbo to Mike, but he had to admit it was impressive.

'Exscuse me,' he whispered, as he pushed in beside a woman who had a baby at her breast. On the other side of her Rosa was not far away and he grinned at her. She raised a fan across her face, perhaps to conceal a smile. The priest droned on. It sure was a curious place. The Virgin was in the fashion of the sixteenth century, a high ruff collar to her dress, her doll-like Son in one hand. The woman nudged Mike and offered him the puking, bellowing brat to hold while she tucked away one breast and brought out the other. Morgan was relieved when the infant was back at the milkbar. He caught Rosa's eye and saw her smiling at his discomfiture. He raised his eyes to the rafters and shrugged.

'Hi,' he said, after the service as she stepped into her carriage. 'How about coming for a stroll?'

'That is impossible.' The duenna intervened as the carriage started away. 'Go away or I will inform the *rurales* that you molest us.'

'I only wanna be friendly,' Morgan said, watching them go. He looked around and saw a group of mariachi players among the folk outside church. 'I ain't finished yet.'

For a small sum the leading player was only too pleased to lead him to the town house of Don Emilio. It was an imposing building faced with Spanish blue and white tiles. By the time they got there the coach had passed through its arched gateway which was firmly closed. Like most Mexican houses a window was open to the air but was stoutly barred. Mike took a stance outside and instructed, 'Right, boys, start playin' and singin'. I want a nice love lament.'

Aptly known as the Enemies of Silence the mariachi band did not hesitate, launching into a guitar-strumming, flute-and-drum accompaniment to their high-pitched voices.

'Ay-yai-yai!' The duenna appeared at the window. 'What's all the noise about?'

But Rosa was at her elbow, whispering in her ear, and urging her away. She herself took a seat and listened until the cacophony ceased.

'How about that?' Morgan said. 'My apology for disturbing your li'l party t'other night. The name's Mike. I'm in partnership with your old man.'

'My father?' She seemed surprised by his informality. 'Yes, I know. I do not think he approves of you.'

'Is he home?'

'No, he had business to attend to.'

'So, *señorita*, how about letting me in? I ain't used to talkin' to a gal from out in the street.'

Rosa gave a worried frown, starting to shake her head, then shrugged and exclaimed, 'Oh, why not? We can take coffee. Only for a little while, then you must go.'

'Good for you. A gal who knows her own mind.' A small door in the great gate of studded oak was opened and he was beckoned inside. Rosa led him into a spacious, Moorish patio amid shady palms beside a fountain-trickling pool. She settled herself at a small table and indicated an adjacent chair for him. 'So, what is so important you wish to speak to me?'

'Waal, ain't that obvious?' He reached out and took her hand. Her fingers were soft and delicate beneath his sunburned, work-roughened ones. 'I guess I've kinda fallen for ya. Didn't they explain that in the song?'

Rosa gave him a radiant smile but snatched her fingers away when the duenna bustled in and started shrilly scolding her. She was eventually persuaded to go away but the girl told him, 'She says you can stay only for five minutes. She is not as fierce as she looks.'

'In that case I ain't got no time to lose.' Morgan got to his feet, caught hold of her in his strong arms, raised her up and planted his lips on hers. At first she struggled like a trapped bird, but then she relaxed and her fingers closed tight about his shoulders as she surrendered to the strange, first-time sensation of a man's kiss.

'Whoo!' Mike gasped. 'I've bin wantin' to do that since I first set eyes on ya.'

Suddenly there was a leather-shod footfall on the flags. Don Emilio had let himself into his house unannounced. His features registered shock and disgust as he stared at them and shouted, 'What the devil is going on? What are you doing with this man? What is he doing in my house?'

Surprised and flustered, Rosa tried to reply. 'This is Señor Morgan. I — '

'I am quite aware who it is. Go to your room, Rosa. Immediately! I will speak to you later.'

'I'm not a child, Father. You can't order me — '

Don Emilio stamped his foot. 'Do as I say, girl.'

There were tears in her eyes as she turned to go and Morgan tried to butt in. 'Hey, there's no need for this. There's no harm done. It was my fault. I was too fast off the mark.'

'Get out of my house, sir.' Don Emilio turned to him with a snarl. 'Or I will have you thrown out. I ought to have you flogged.'

'Yeah? Well, I wouldn't try that if I were you.'

Morgan backed away however, as two manservants came towards him. 'OK, I'm going, don't worry, pal. I'm on my way. We'll talk about it, señor, maybe when you've calmed down.'

'Don't count on it,' Don Emilio snapped, pointing a finger accusingly at him. 'If you ever try to touch my daughter again you will be a dead man.'

4

'What's that flea-bitten thang you got 'tween your knees?' Rowdy guffawed, when he saw Morgan riding up the cobbled street on his newly acquired mule.

'I'd back this mule aginst a racehorse any day,' Mike replied. 'Over two hundred miles. Everythang's relative, as the man said.'

'Where ya off to?'

'Hunting,' he sang out, as he jogged past.

The truth was there had been little choice along at the corral. A few knock-kneed nags who had had the spirit ground out of them. The 300 years of the most cruel colonial rule since the Romans had seen *peons* banned from owning a horse, or a gun, along with other prohibitions such as the right to cultivate the vine. The result was that the landowners kept the finest mustangs for their *vaqueros*. To drown their sorrows the common people drank vile cactus-juice, or pulque beer made from the maguey plant.

'It's one hell of a country,' Morgan muttered as he forced a passage through the crowds: barefoot children, ragged peasants, deformed beggars, sorceresses selling 'cure-alls', an old man prostrate on the church steps flaying his own bleeding back. 'Funny thang is they all seem happy, at least for today.' Maybe the mescal or the five per cent proof pulque had something to do with that.

At the Santa Rosa railroad depot he claimed his trunk from the left luggage, opened it up and took out the accoutrements of the rodeo rider: cowhide chaps, gloves, spurs, and a fancy red bandanna, which would serve as a dust mask. It was all practical wear for the trail, and he attired himself carefully, donning a fringed buckskin jacket, creased but comfortable. He pulled out his soogans, his rubber-backed bedroll and his Winchester carbine. He loaded twelve bullets into the magazine and tucked a dozen-box of .44s into his jacket pocket. Lastly, with something akin to awe he uncovered the silver-inlaid Smith & Wesson, in its bullet-studded gunbelt. He spun the cylinder and loaded it with six of the .44s.

The luggage attendant watched him curiously as he rolled his soogans around the Winchester and tied the pack behind his saddle. Then he jerked his gunbelt a notch tighter. 'Last time I used this in anger was at the Horsehead Crossing when we got attacked by two hundred screaming Comanches,' he explained in Spanish. 'We were herding up the Pecos trail to Cheyenne, but I guess that's outa your territory.'

The man laughed. 'There are no Comanches around here, señor.'

'No, but there's other varmints.' He swung onto the mule and patted the S. & W. in its holster. 'This is my insurance policy. *Gracias, señor. Adios.*'

'*Vaya con Dios*,' the man called after him.

'Yeah, maybe I'll need a little of his help,' Morgan muttered, as he set the mule's nose towards the mountains. 'Come on, you ornery bastard, let's move.'

It was good to get away from the dust, noise, filth and flies of the town, even if it was a bit of a jerky ride, the mule going with a stiff-legged gait, braying in protest at the spurs, but settling into a fair pace. He followed the trail out of town, casting off from the more direct route of their new railroad. There were smallholdings with dusty orange-trees, patches of maize and spikes of maguey. Scraggy turkeys and hens scattered as he passed and hid beneath the twisted agaves.

'*Buenos!*' He returned the abbreviated greeting of a *peon* in cotton pyjamas coming late into town on his burro, his wife walking behind with a huge bundle on her head. The donkey would be his most precious possession, more valuable than a woman. So in Mexico the burro carried the man, the woman the load. They were the only traffic he encountered. Most of the population were at the fiesta, excitedly awaiting the next day's bullfight.

It was midsummer; the sun blazed from a clear blue sky, but at 4,000 feet or so it was cool and pleasant on this fertile plateau. The only cloud haloed the volcano, which seemed to hang malevolently over them, but was in fact, far distant, its flat snowy cap protruding above the mist.

Soon the fields gave way to more rocky terrain and the trail wound towards an imposing, high-walled hacienda. This ranch house was the home, he had been told, of Don Emilio, whose lands stretched for miles on along the plateau — 100,000 acres, 5,000 head of cattle, and hundreds of horses and mules.

'It looks more like a fort than a home,' Morgan muttered to himself as he spotted an armed guard in a watchtower. He abandoned the trail, intending to bypass the hacienda and headed across grasslands where knots of cattle were grazing. But two horsemen came from its outer gate and weaved their way through the cows at a fast lope until they confronted him. Each of the *vaqueros* had a rifle in his hand; they were stern-faced in greasy range clothes and ornate sombreros. 'What do you want here?' one shouted as the other took an aggressive stance behind him. 'Who are you?'

'I'm building the railroad,' Morgan drawled in his frontier Spanish. 'Don Emilio has given us permission to survey the land.'

The one blocking his path studied him, quizzically. 'Don Emilio has said nothing to us about this.'

'No, I don't suppose he has because he's in town.' Mike grinned as he spoke the half-truth. 'I can assure you I been having words with him. I want to take a look at this country in case we have to change our route.'

The *vaquero* gave a shrill cackle of laughter. 'You dress like a *charro*, not a railroadman.' Hawklike, he eyed the revolver on Morgan's hip. 'You look like a bad *hombre*, gringo.'

'No, my intentions are entirely peaceful,' Mike said. 'Can I go on my way?'

'Sure, but watch out for the bulls. They are dangerous.'

'Yup. I've been around bulls. I guess I can handle 'em. So long, boys.'

He spurred the mule into the semblance of a trot and went charging away. He heard the *vaqueros'* laughter borne on the wind as the mule kicked and brayed. 'Guess we do make an odd couple,' he said.

* * *

'It was a terrible shock to me,' Don Emilio said, 'to find my daughter in the arms of a drunken, brawling lout. To see you — no, I cannot bear to repeat in words what I saw, but you know what you were doing.'

'You have got the wrong idea about it, about Mike Morgan.'

'I do not have the wrong idea,' he went on in his quiet but severe manner. 'It is you who have the wrong idea. Last night you saw him, yourself, with those street sluts, drunkenly disgracing himself in the hotel.'

Rosa had been summoned to her father's study in the town house and was standing before him like some schoolgirl. 'I doubt,' she murmured, 'if he is the first man in Mexico to have made use of vendable ladies.'

'What? You try to excuse him? How could you not know better than to invite a man like that into my house behind my back, to allow him to embrace you?'

'It is also my house.'

'If you have no respect for my wishes, perhaps you should remember it was the home of your mother and you might treat it with the respect her memory should be accorded. What is the matter with you, Rosa? Have you forgotten everything I have taught you?'

He sat behind his fine desk in the ornate room with its high French ceiling, its elaborate moulding. In a lacquered cabinet behind him were displayed silver plate and rare china vases. The heavy curtains of the study were made of rich tapestry to shield them from the harsh sunlight. It seemed to the girl that her father, as he toyed with a silver inkwell, lived in a more rarefied world than the everyday one outside.

'Have you no respect for the memory of your grandfather, for your family bloodline going back over six generations, connected to Spanish royalty?'

Oh, my grandfather? She might have known that he would mention that incident. The times she had been told that horror story were uncountable, how he had been slashed to pieces by the rebels' machetes, his severed head nailed to the front gate of the hacienda, how their land had been seized and they were allowed to retain only this town house during the years when a full-blooded Indian, Benito Juárez, was president of Mexico. Her father had been in the army, fighting alongside the French. When they were toppled the Emperor Maximilian was put up against a wall and shot. His own life had only been saved by the intervention of his old schoolfriend, Captain Porfirio Díaz, a turncoat who had joined the rebels.

'You are too young to know the suffering we had to bear, and I am glad you were. Why, we had to allow common peasants to have rooms here. The mess they made was indescribable.'

'I really see nothing wrong with the ideas of Juárez — free schools and hospitals, divide the land among the poor,' she said, surprised at her own temerity. 'He was a true Christian trying to help the downtrodden.'

'Oh, my God!' Don Emilio put his hand to his forehead in a gesture of horror. 'What are you saying? Have you become one of *them*? Don't you realize you are betraying your own class, your own family, by saying such things? I cannot believe it. We have to stick together, Rosa, or we are all doomed. We have had twenty years of peace under Don Porfirio but there is revolution in the air again. A bandit in the north, Pancho Villa, is causing mayhem. He killed a *haciendado's* son. I cannot understand why he is not hunted down and shot.'

Yes, Porfirio Diaz had wheedled his way into Juárez's trust, all the while plotting with men such as her father to seize power when he died. Soon they had the Indians and *peons* under their iron rule again. The land was returned to the generals and ruling class. Priests, who had been defrocked and persecuted, if not shot, were reinstated, and looted silver, gold and lands returned to the church.

'There is no freedom in this country,' Rosa ventured. 'One day the bubbling cauldron of hatred and fear will boil over. Diaz can not go on for ever.'

'You don't understand,' her father cried. 'The peasants had no idea what to do with the land when they were given it. They are ignorant, superstitious brutes. All this talk of equality is foolish. Men are not equal. Some are born to rule and others to slave. That's the way the world is. Thank God there is nobody else present to hear what you say, Rosa. Don't you understand? Your words are treasonable.'

'I don't care,' she replied, stubbornly. 'I don't have such a bad picture of humanity as you, father.'

'Enough! What we are here to discuss is this Yankee reprobate, Morgan. I insist that you promise never to speak to him again, or attempt to see him.'

'I cannot make that promise.'

'Don't you understand that I am trying to protect you? You must know that any marriageable girl in Mexico must be a virgin. All the more so among people of our high rank. We have to set the example. You will have no more thoughts of this drifter, this wildcatter, this cowboy, Morgan. You must cut him out of your life for ever. You must make up your mind to marry a suitable man of culture and wealth, one of us, a man of high-standing. It is your duty to the Fatherland.'

'Duty?' she faltered.

'Duty, yes, to your family, too. We have little time. We must dress for the ball. You will take your place alongside me in the position of honour where all can admire your beauty and grace. You will be the centre of all eyes. Surely then you will see that you must never disgrace yourself again.'

'I don't consider I have. It was only a little kiss.'

'It is what that might lead to. Go now. By the way, I have dismissed your duenna.'

'What?' Rosa spun around at the door. 'How could you? It was not her fault.'

'She disobeyed my strict orders, let

you make a fool of yourself. It is too late to protest. She has been thrown out, bag and baggage.' Don Emiliano fluttered his fingers, dismissively. 'Go!'

★ ★ ★

Morgan rode the mule hard for most of the day across the rocky landscape until, as the sun began its descent, he reached the outer rim of the plateau and followed it along, searching for a path down to the plain. At a vantage point he jumped down, took a slim telescope from his pocket, extended it and squinted down to where a silver ribbon of river snaked, glinting golden in the sunset. 'Yup,' he grunted, spotting what might be a work gang, smoke rising from their camp. 'That could be 'em.'

The evening silence of the great plateau was broken by the sound of tinkling bells and men's voices and he turned to see a mule train picking its way down through a steep *barranca*.

The leading *arriero*, or mule driver, was a weather-beaten old man of mixed race, probably Negro-Indian, his hair and beard a curly grizzled grey. '*Hola!*' he called, and spoke in an Indian patois to his men. He had peddled tin kettles, gunpowder and machetes among the mountain villages and was returning with woven goods.

'Is there a path down to the valley?' Morgan asked, offering cigarettes to the man and his fellow-drivers.

More by sign-language than words, as they gathered around him, he managed to convey his question and the fact that he was an engineer. 'Are they building a railroad down there?'

'Ah, *sí, sí*.' The muleteer grinned as he savoured the tobacco, and made a charade of knocking in spikes. 'Not good. You put me out of business, eh?'

'How long would it take me to get down there?'

The leader, in his ragged topcoat and leggings, clambered to the edge of the rim and pointed to a cliff of steep shale plunging almost vertically down to the base of the valley. 'One hour, maybe two. You go down faster than you come up, if you make it and your animal don't break leg.'

Morgan screwed up his eyes with disbelief. It looked an extremely dangerous descent, especially as the sun was sinking away into the far-distant Pacific ocean and the light was fast fading. 'Are you joking?'

'You cheeken, meester? OK, you come with us. Take six hours to river. *Mañana*. Tonight we camp here.'

When Mike told him his name, he grinned some more. 'You Miguel? Me Miguel, too. We brothers. Come, we make fire, we eat.'

Morgan saw no reason not to camp out with them; they were honest traders, not bandits, unlikely to try to cut his throat or rob him in the night. So he shared their pot of *frijoles* and sweaty goat-cheese in exchange for his tobacco. Miguel spoke a crude Spanish, but the others conversed in an Indian dialect, one of many that changed from valley to valley in the mountains. They laughed a lot, getting merrier as they passed around a goatskin of *aguardiente*. Morgan winced as he took a mouthful.

At last, as the stars came out and the fire fell into embers, they wrapped themselves in their serapes and the silence of the night was broken only by their snores and the tinkle of mule bells. Morgan lay awake for a while and thought about the girl, Rosa. Her radiant beauty had knocked him off of his feet, as they say. But he had played his cards wrong, upset Don Emilio. 'No, there ain't no future in it. We live in different worlds,' he muttered, pulling his Stetson down over his face to cut out the moon's stark glare. 'I gotta fergit them Spanish eyes of her'n.'

5

'*Adios, amigos,*' Morgan yelled, as he sat back deep in the saddle and plunged on the mule down the steep escarpment, ploughing through soft scree, hauling the animal around boulders and leaping on again into a dizzying descent. Down, down, down they went, like skiers on snow which he had heard about. It was too late to stop now, an exhilaration thrilled in him as they were propelled on down the almost vertical cliff until they suddenly reached rock-bottom a mile or so below. 'Yee-hoo!' he whooped 'That sure beats bull-riding!'

The mule, too, seemed pleased with himself, raising his head proudly, and letting out a triumphant bray as he trotted away through the giant cacti, eroded rocks and mesquite. 'Come on, boy, we've made it,' Mike urged, leaning forward to pat its neck. 'Now let's find that durn railroad.'

* * *

A gang of coolies were busy pounding down the bed of a track they had laid following the edge of the meandering Rio Tinto. Morgan appraised their efforts with a professional eye as he approached. The track was too close to the river for his liking. But the Chinese were renowned for being fast, brave and efficient workers. Cheap labour, too.

'Howdy,' he drawled to a rotund fellow in a concertinaed top hat and a once-snazzy waistcoat, who was wielding the customary club of the gang boss. 'How ya doin'?'

'What's it to you?' Beefy and bull-necked, the American swung his club suspiciously. 'Where'n hell you come from, anyhow?'

'Aw, jest passin' by. Lost all my dough in a monte game, so I'm lookin' fer work. How much you pay?'

'Three pesos a day to these monkeys. It wouldn't be any good to you.'

'What's that? Fifty cents. Nope, it ain't a lot, is it?' Morgan offered a cigarette and looked around at the piles of rails, machinery, and the portable huts of the camp. 'How much track you lay in a day?'

'Sixteen miles on a good day.' The gang boss grinned as he struck a match. 'That's with me behind 'em larupping a few butts.'

'Waal, maybe I could speak to your top man, see what other kinda work you got. Where is he?'

'He ain't here. They're back at the coast, building a jetty, and dredging the estuary.'

'So, you ain't goin' through Puerto?'

'Nope, this is an independent operation. We're going the long, easy route, up across the side of the volcano and taking the gradual ascent up to the mines. When we get the contract for the tin we'll ship it out via the estuary.'

Morgan gave a whistle as he sat the

mule and took a drag of his cigarette. 'You K and T boys sure know how to git ahead.'

'We ain't K an' T. We're California and Gulf. New company.' The gang boss smirked proudly. 'Sure, we know what we're doing. Not like them other stupid bastards.'

'Yeah? Who are they?'

'Aw, a coupla wildcatters. They think they can run a railroad up from Santa Rosa straight through the damn mountains.'

'So, can't they?'

'I can tell you, brother,' the man growled, slapping his club in his palm, 'those crazy guys ain't got a snowball in hell's chance of gettin' there before us. We'll make sure of that.'

'You don't say? You plannin' on playin' rough an' dirty, are ya?'

'Hey, what's it to you?' The man tipped his tophat over one eye and scratched the back of his head, perplexed. 'Who the hell are you?'

Morgan shrugged and turned the

mule away, ambling along to the Chinese who were swinging their sledge-hammers in unison as two more rails went down. 'Hey, you men,' he shouted. 'Howdja like to work for me? I'm paying six pesos a day.' He dug a silver dollar from his pocket and held it up. 'Or one of these fer each of you every day.'

The coolies, in their rags and straw-hats, ceased work, regarded him and started jabbering among themselves in their own lingo. 'Where this work, mister?' an older one asked.

'We're building a track up in the hills.' Morgan pointed back into the distance. 'You wanna come with me?'

'Silver dollar a day?'

'That's our rate, Irishman, Indian, or whoever. But I should warn you, it could be dangerous work.'

'Hey, what's going on?' The gang boss blundered in and started belabouring the coolies with his club. 'Y'all get back to work, you hear?' He turned to Morgan, the club raised and started foul-mouthing him. 'What you playing at? You a damn troublemaker? I thought you said you wanted work.'

'No, you musta misheard. I want workers. Didn't I introduce myself? I'm one of them crazy bastards up in the hills.'

The man's jaw dropped and he turned and hurried back to one of the sheds.

'Look out, mister. He go for gun.'

'Yeah, I kinda guessed he might.' Morgan spurred the mule after the man, drawing his revolver. 'Don't do nuthin' stupid, Beefy,' he shouted. 'This is fair trade. They're entitled to come with me. No need for that language, neither. That's very insulting to my mother!'

But, cursing a blue streak, the gang boss burst from the shed, a sawn-off shotgun in his hands. Was it a threat? Or was he going to fire? Morgan didn't wait to find out. He squeezed his trigger first and the S & W's bullet seared across the man's right wrist. The shotgun exploded simultaneously as he screamed and dropped it.

The mule shied away and when he turned back Morgan spurred him up close and smashed the American across his jaw with the revolver butt. 'Yeah, think yourself lucky ye've only lost a couple of bad teeth,' he growled. 'Next time you aim a scattergun at me you better be sayin' your prayers.'

He left the gang boss lying on the ground, wiping blood from his mouth. 'OK, boys, grab your bedrolls. Let's be on our way. I wanna make the top of the plateau well 'fore sundown.' He grinned at the older man who spoke English. 'You better bring that shotgun along. We may be needing it.'

★ ★ ★

Doña Cleminia del Haste de Terrazos was, at eighty, an imposing old lady who tried to retain a rod-of-iron rule over her son's hacienda. When her husband's head had been severed by the blood-thirsty revolutionaries her life had been spared. But when their lands had been returned to them by Don Porfirio she had dedicated herself to vengeful support of the new regime.

With her long silver hair wound into a bun on top of her nobly Spanish head, held by a diamond tiara, her earlobes elongated by years of supporting dangling jewels, a capacious silken dress covering her now ancient body, she spent much of her day tracing her family's lineage back to the days of Cortes' conquest.

Today she was occupied with the eighteen different mestizo gradations ranging between pure-blood Spaniards at the pinnacle, down through Spanish-Indian, Spanish-Negro, Indian-Negro, to pure-blood Indians lowest of all. It troubled her that the latest prospective bridegroom she had chosen for Rosa appeared to have a taint of Indian in his Spanish blood. She sighed for it was not unexpected. Very few Spanish women

73

had been brought over by the early colonists.

Nor did the family of Ferdinand Lopez possess a great deal of land or money. They had lost it in some scandal years before. But Ferdinand had been sent away to business school in North America, he spoke English and French, and her son seemed to think he was a suitable suitor for the girl.

'So, how did you get on with Ferdinand at the ball last night?' she asked when Rosa came into the room.

'Oh?' Rosa shrugged. 'He's OK, if you don't mind having your toes stepped on.'

'Your father thinks you are well-matched. Personally, he is not the man I would have wished for you. But he is a go-getter. He should do well if your father guides him, takes him into business.'

'He's not my sort, for God's sake, grandmother!' Rosa was exasperated at the way they were trying to marry her off. 'I'm not in love with him.'

'That's not important!' the old woman snapped. 'How many times must I tell you that a wife's role is modesty and obedience to her husband. You would learn to love him and your children.'

Oh, Ferdinand was a go-getter, all right, Rosa thought, recalling how he had inveigled her out onto the veranda at the ball, roughly had tried to kiss her, his hands brutally roaming everywhere, he gutturally vowing his love as he did so. None of it rang true. It was obvious that he saw her as a doorway to her father's money.

'No, it's out of the question. I can't stand him.' She had been out in the courtyard gardening at the raised beds — raised so that ladies wouldn't need to bend their backs. She took off her muddy gloves and arranged cut flowers in a vase. 'We are on the cusp of the twentieth century, grandmother. I think I have the right to choose my own husband.'

'In that case we must send you away

to Mexico City to mix in higher society. You will find a decent suitor there,' the old lady decreed. 'A pity. At least Ferdinand is from Santa Rosa, one of us.'

'I don't want to go to Mexico City,' Rosa groaned. 'Don't you understand?'

'So, it's true, is it? I hardly dared believe it of you. You have set your cap at this Texan reprobate, this railroad fly-by-night. I absolutely forbid it. I agree with your father. You must never be allowed to see that man again. Now go to your room and change your dress for luncheon. Then you must get ready for the bullfight this afternoon. The governor will be there.'

'Oh, bother dresses,' Rosa whispered as she left the room. 'I am sick of changing dresses six times a day, of being watched and not allowed to put a foot out of place.' Her father seemed to regard her as his creation, to be cosseted like one of the sickly orchids he tended in his glasshouse.

'What are you muttering about, girl?'

demanded her new duenna, a stout old tyrant. 'Come now, where is your maid?'

My new jailer, Rosa thought, and said aloud, 'Perhaps it's time a few glasshouse windows were broken. I feel as though I'm stifling.'

'What nonsense you do talk,' the duenna said, leading her to her bedroom. 'I'll have to report this.'

But all Rosa could think of as she was changed, had her hair brushed until it shone, was Mike Morgan, the touch of his lips on hers. 'I'm obsessed by him,' she whispered. 'Oh, I can't help it. I must see him again.'

★ ★ ★

'Waal, lookee who's here,' Lefty crowed, scratching at his unshaven jaw, his greasy hat shading his eyes as he peered over the edge of the ravine. 'Who the hell's that lot climbing up behind him?'

'What?' Hank Pike climbed from his mustang and knelt beside him, raising a pair of binoculars. 'Those are our coolies, dammit. There's the old one, their leader, what's his name?'

'Ho. That fella Morgan's stole 'em. Or they're deserting.'

'Well, it ain't gonna be ho ho ho for him. What do they do with deserters?'

'They shoot 'em.' Lefty licked his lips as he levered his carbine. 'That's what they do.'

'Hold it,' Hank said. 'Maybe that would be a bit drastic. It'd bring the *rurales* up here. No, I got a better idea. We'll make this look like an accident. See that?' He nodded to a big pile of rocks hanging over the narrow ravine. 'They're just waitin' to be dislodged.'

Morgan had led the coolies up the twisting mule path from the plain, meeting Miguel and his *arrieros* as they were coming down. They had exchanged a few words, Miguel describing how if they crossed the grassy plateau, looking out for landmarks, they could cut up through a ravine into the higher mountains. It would save them a big diversion back to Santa Rosa. If they bore right at a fork it would lead to their railroad camp.

'*Gracias, amigo*,' Mike called, and squeezed past the mules, leading his new workers on up the zigzagging precipitous trail until they reached the plateau.

It was not difficult to follow the trail of the mule train. They were occasionally approached by *vaqueros* out herding Don Emilio's cattle. But it seemed there was an ancient right of way across the plateau to reach the mountain villages so they did not offer any threat.

It was well past high noon when they made their way up a steep-sided *barranca*, taking it steady because of the high altitude but pressing on, for Mike wanted to try to reach his camp before nightfall. He had allowed the boys a short break to cook up rice in their pots and refresh themselves at a fast-running stream. But they were a cheerful bunch, in their rags, bare-legged, in sandals, and eager to follow him, so he remounted his mule and led the way.

Suddenly, some instinct of self-preservation made him look up. He caught a glimpse of a man on the ridge with a pole in his hands levering at a pile of rocks. 'Jeez!' he gulped as the rocks began to move. 'Run for it, boys.'

The Chinese looked upwards with horrified expressions as they saw great boulders bearing down on top of them, bouncing and twisting, gathering more as they came. They didn't need second telling: screaming, pushing and leaping back down the steep path, as the landslide in its dust cloud crashed down upon them . . .

★   ★   ★

It was as if Rosa's whole body and soul were beating with emotion, possessing her mind, overcoming all reason. Escape! Get away! She had been imprisoned in this high-walled ranch house all her life. She felt like a bird beating its wings against the bars of its cage. She had to go to him, the man who had aroused this strange passion in her, tell him of her love, discover — she had to know — if he felt the same way about her.

'I am going to take a siesta,' she told her duenna, pressing her bedroom door shut in her face. 'I would like to be alone.'

Quickly, Rosa changed into a white starched blouse, split leather skirt and riding-boots, tucking her hair under a stiff-brimmed hat. She clutched her whip, and carefully climbed from the veranda, hanging onto the fronds of a bougainvillaea until she reached the courtyard. The duenna would be sitting in a chair outside her room, watching and waiting. Too bad for her.

The house was quiet; masters and staff were enjoying a respite from the heat of the day. Rosa made her way to the stables and saddled her stallion, Blaze. Officially termed a grey he was more the colour of milk. He was a proud, feisty beast; the girl was the only one he would let near him without kicking and biting. She hushed his whinnied greeting, calling out to a startled groom that she was going for a ride, and to open the stable door. He was a big horse, all of seventeen hands, but she managed to gain the saddle and once aboard, her feet in the stirrups, she felt more in command. 'Come on,' she cried, steering him out and towards the outer gate in the wall. 'Open up!' she commanded. 'Hurry!'

Free! She touched spurs to the flanks of the magnificent stallion and rejoiced to feel him pounding beneath her, his mane blowing in her face as she leaned over his muscular neck urging him into a gallop, speeding away across the plain. 'Go, Blaze,' she called. 'Go.'

Of course, it would be unwise to keep that pace up for long. She had a long way to go. She planned to ride across the plateau until she reached the old muleteers' trail. If she headed up through the gulch she was pretty sure it would lead her to the railroad camp. She needed to get there before sundown. So, although she eased pressure, she kept Blaze going at a steady lope.

'Oh, no,' she groaned as she saw one of her father's more trusted *vaqueros*, Jorge, spot her and leave a bunch of bulls he was escorting to ride across, bull-lance in hand. He caught her up and charged along by her side. 'I don't need company,' she called. 'I'm just going for an afternoon ride.'

'But, Señorita Rosa, I cannot allow you to go alone,' he shouted. 'It is more than my life is worth.'

'Don't be ridiculous.' She snorted. 'I'm not a child. Just go and get on with your work. I need some solitude. I'll be back before dark.'

But the rugged *vaquero* on his wiry mustang was not to be shaken off and went dashing along by her side. 'Permit me, *señorita*, I must accompany you. Those are my orders. There is danger. What if you fall? What if you run into bulls? What if there are bandits about?'

'Yes, what if a black jaguar leaps at me,' she scoffed. 'That would serve me

83

right, eh? Go away. Leave me.'

When she glanced around, however, although he had dropped back fifty yards, he was determinedly trailing her. 'Oh, God,' she said. Maybe, if she waited her chance she could outrun him. 'Come on, Blaze,' she yelled. '*Vamos!*'

★ ★ ★

When the dust cleared Morgan heard the screams and groans of the injured, but he was more interested in the men glimpsed at the top of the escarpment as the last stone of the landslide rolled to a halt. One had disappeared behind the ridge, but the other, a tall man, in Stetson and long riding-coat, was standing silhouetted against the red sky of the setting sun, a carbine in his hand.

'It's that varmint, Hank Pike, sure enough,' Morgan muttered. He had dragged his mule higher up the path to escape the landslide. He pulled his Winchester from the bedroll, levered a slug into the magazine, tugged it into his shoulder and fired off three shots in fast succession. 'Dammit, missed.'

The attacker had dodged back behind the cover of a boulder, but Mike glimpsed the glint of his carbine barrel and jumped for cover himself. Just in time. Chips of rock splintered about his head as bullets whined and ricocheted. Morgan remembered that the American desperado had been carrying a Spencer, so he waited until seven were spent, then leaped forward, climbing up the steep cliffside as fast as he could.

It was a hard climb and he paused half-way, out of breath. He spotted Hank moving stealthily away so let him have another volley of lead. The tall man leapt for his life like a startled rabbit and rolled away over the ridge as the echos of the explosions bounced off the *barranca*'s walls.

Mike Morgan listened but there was only the whine of the mountain wind, an eagle slowly spiralling up in the sky.

He guessed they had made a run for it. No point in trying to climb to the top. So he ploughed back down to rejoin the Chinese who were jabbering incomprehensibly to him.

'Waal, I warned ya it could be dangerous, didn't I?' he drawled, as he knelt to examine a coolie crushed beneath a huge rock. He tried the neck pulse of his grief-stricken face, but there was no go. 'He ain't gonna be drawin' his pay.'

Another was bleeding profusely from a head gash, yet others were dishevelled and groaning at minor injuries, and one looked as though he'd got a bad case of cracked ribs. 'It ain't as bad as I feared,' Morgan said to the man called Ho. 'I'm goin' after them murderers.'

Maybe it was a fool's errand. The shadows were already lengthening. But he got on the mule and set off back down the pass. Maybe he could cut them off, maybe not.

★ ★ ★

It was almost dark, the sun had fallen away beyond the plateau ridge as Rosa galloped the white stallion across the grassland, swerving to the east when she spotted the steep-sided *barranca* leading up through banks of pine-trees darkly clothing the lower slopes of the mountains. 'That's the way,' she said to herself. 'I'm certain. Come on, Blaze. Go!'

She had been riding horses since the age of five and was a fine, agile equestrienne, although her father tried to discourage her. It was unsafe, he said, and unladylike. She glanced back and smiled with satisfaction to see that there was no sign of Jorge as she started up the slope. She must have covered at least fifteen miles from the hacienda and there was that much again to go before she reached the railroad camp. What, she wondered, with some apprehension, should she do if she were caught out in this mountain wilderness alone in the dark?

As the shadows of the pines closed

about her she was startled to hear the sound of gunshots clattering through the mule-pass up ahead. What was going on? Who could it be? Hunters? Or worse?

Rosa reined in, wondering whether it might be best to hide in the woods for a while. But she had come unprepared to camp out. Probably they were just muleteers shooting their supper or having target practice. Best to press on.

Blaze was a big horse with a big heart and went charging on up the well-trodden path. A forty-mile ride out did not bother him in the least. But suddenly he paused, pricking up his ears and peering ahead into the gloom.

Two riders were coming fast towards them and she could take no evading action before they burst out of the trees.

'Hey, who's this?' A tall man, in a wide-brimmed hat and duster coat, called out, as he swirled his mustang around beside her.

His tubbier sidekick had hauled in

hard in front of her, blocking her way. 'Whooee! A cute l'il honey, ain't she?' An evil grin split his coarse features as he put out a hand and caught hold of Rosa's reins. 'Not so fast, missy. What's your hurry?'

'Get out of my way, you fool.' Rosa was unused to being spoken to in this manner. And to tell the truth she was frightened. There was something about these two she did not like the look of. Desperate to escape she slashed her riding-quirt across the man's face and spurred Blaze forwards.

She could hear the riders whooping as they pursued her, as if this was some game. Nor did she get far. A lariat noose landed about her shoulders, jerked tight, and she was torn abruptly from her saddle to land with an uncomfortable thump in the dust.

'Hold still, you bastard,' the shorter man shouted, cursing the whinnying, kicking stallion as he dragged it back to them by its reins. 'This is some hoss. We could get two hundred dollars for him.

He's got the devil in him, but I'll soon kick some sense into his brain.'

'Yeah, the gal ain't so bad, either,' his companion drawled as he watched Rosa climb painfully to her feet. He gave a jerk of the lariat to tighten it around her shoulders and pulled her to him. 'Waal, beautiful? What shall we do with ya?'

'You lay a finger on me my father will have you both flayed alive,' Rosa warned. 'I advise you to let me go and I'll be on my way.'

'Your father? Who's he?'

'Don Emilio Terrazos.' Rosa haughtily tossed her dark hair out of her eyes, aware of her exalted position. 'You have heard of him, surely?'

'Don Emilio, huh?' The tall man scratched at his unshaven jaw. 'The *mucho* rich landowner who's backing our competition. Well, well, whadda ya know, Lefty? How much you reckon this Don Emilio would pay ransom to get his daughter back?'

'Ya mean after we've had our fun

with her?' Lefty rubbed his burning cheek. 'Feisty li'l bitch, ain't she? She's jest askin' fer it, ain't she, Hank?'

'Yep, a pure, white-skinned thoroughbred, like her hoss. Jest the sort I like an' ain't had in a long time.' Hank Pike jerked the girl close to him, and, with his free hand grabbed at her breast, tearing her blouse. Rosa screamed shrilly, and tried to fight away from him. 'We'll git a damn sight more for this honey than the California and Gulf is paying us.'

'Yeah, we'll be rich,' Lefty giggled, leaning from his *bronco*, to grab a handful of Rosa's luxuriant hair, jerking her back towards him. 'Let's take her up into the woods, *amigo*.'

'You keep ya filthy hands off'n her.' Hank jerked Rosa up off the ground by the rope and put an arm around her waist, hauling her to him. 'I take first poke at her. Yessir. Ain't no use struggling, gal.'

But, suddenly, the stallion, incensed by the attack on the girl, was up on his hind-legs, pawing the air with steel-shod hoofs, kicking out at Lefty on his mustang, who cursed and slashed his iron-tipped whip across the horse's face. 'Git back you brute,' he howled in alarm.

He howled more when a bull lance came hissing through the air and buried its steel head deep in his entrails. He was tumbled to the ground, to lie kicking and gasping like a landed fish.

As the Mexican, Jorge, appeared out of the falling darkness, Pike dropped the girl, hauled out a long-barrelled revolver, levelled it at the *vaquero*, and fired. There was the flash of the explosion and Rosa screamed again. She crawled over to Jorge as he lay on the ground in a pool of blood. 'You've killed him,' she groaned.

'No, have I?' Hank grinned with mock surprise. 'Waal, he skewered my pal, so it's tit for tat. An' talking about tit' — he jerked the lariat tight again — 'git on your hoss, whore. You're comin' with me.'

But Hank was rattled, peering into the dusk from where the Mexican had come, wondering if there were any more with him. Noticing that he was looking away, Rosa tried, stealthily, to reach for Jorge's knife in his boot. Hank spotted her and jerked her back on her feet. 'Nice try, bitch. I don't trust you. You're gonna ride in front. Anybody tries anythang you gonna git it first. So git on Lefty's hoss. Or would you prefer to be dragged?'

'Maybe she'd prefer you dead?' Morgan's voice rang out from behind, making Pike stop in his tracks.

'Aw, shit,' he groaned. 'I'd forgot about you.'

'Throw that revolver aside, pronto.' Morgan stepped from the pines. 'Toss that rope on the girl away, too.'

Hank whirled his horse around and blasted the sixgun. But Morgan's arm was outstretched, the S & W unwavering in his fist, aiming for a heart shot. Whether he changed his mind, or it was the movement of the horse, but the bullet that blasted out powered through Hank's shoulder as his shot went wild. Slowly, Pike toppled to the ground.

Morgan relieved him of the revolver. 'You'll live,' he growled as the killer grovelled in the dust, clutching at his bloody arm. 'You're gonna make a full confession to your crimes an' who you're working for. The Mexican authorities can hang you and throw Gulf an' California, or whatever they're called, outa the country. You betcha.'

He glanced at Rosa, who was staring at him as if with disbelief. 'You OK, sweetheart?' He eased the noose of rawhide rope from her shoulders. 'First I'll need this to tie this monkey tight 'fore we decide what to do.'

When he had kicked and prodded the injured man over to a pine-bole and secured him, having searched him, tossed away a knife and a small two-shot derringer, he stood and grinned at her in an anxious manner. 'What 'n hell are you doin' out here in the middle of nowhere, anyhow?'

'Mike.' Rosa ran to him, squeezing herself into him, her tears wetting his shirt as she shuddered and gasped out. 'I came to look for you. You . . . you save me from death.'

'Yeah?' He hugged her to him, somewhat perplexed. 'Maybe I saved you from a fate worse than that.'

'*Sí*, those horrible men. The things they say. You came just in time.' She looked up at him, adoringly. 'Darling, I wan' you to know, I can't help it, as soon as I look into your eyes it is like lightning-bolt. I love you.'

'Hey, hold on. Not so fast.' He pointed the S & W at the prostrate Jorge. 'Who's he?'

'One of my father's *vaqueros*. He follow me.'

'You mean you came here alone?'

'*Sí*, of course, I came to tell you of my love, to hear what you have to say.'

'Whoa, Rosa, don't you go flashing them Spanish eyes at me.' But he was weakening as she clung to him. 'We gotta talk about this.'

But it was no good, he couldn't fight her, or the insistent urge she fired in him. 'Well, I'll be jiggered,' he said, hugging her into his strong embrace, as they kissed. And, after a breather, kissed some more.

'Aw, cut it out,' Hank groaned from his tree. 'I can't stand this.'

6

It was too dark, pitch dark, in fact, under the canopy of pine-needles, to either go forwards or back. The moon had yet to rise from behind the high escarpment. 'We might as well take a rest, brew up some cawfee,' Morgan drawled, loose-tethering the mule, the stallion and the two mustangs so they could crop the vegetation. He unhitched his bedroll, and moved away from the trail. 'We'll make a fire up by these rocks.'

'Hey, what about me?' Hank whined, from back in the darkness.

'You can go kiss a coyote.' Morgan fumbled about, building a fireplace of rocks, finding dry kindling, striking a match and soon had a blaze of pine-knots with his coffee-pot hissing and bubbling. He spread his soogans and said, 'Take a pew, Rosa. Relax.'

He figured the Chinese coolies would be cooking up their pots of rice and tending the wounded. 'It ain't much,' he said, handing her a piece of gnarled sausage and a tortilla from his pack, 'but it'll keep us going.'

When she had eaten he passed her his tin mug full of steaming coffee, tossed more dry wood on the fire, and sat beside her, leaning his back against the sun-warmed rock face. 'Waal, Rosa, you sure have put me in a predicament. What'n hail's your father gonna say?'

'I don' care.' The girl shook her head, speaking in broken English. 'He treat me like child. He theenk I must be perfect, like he say my mother was. He put me on, how you say, pedestal. Eet is prison to me. I am stifling in that house. I am not child. I am woman. I am so glad I escape, I find you, Mike.'

Morgan put a fingernail to his teeth to dislodge a tough bit of chorrizo and spat it out. He met her eyes, luminous in the firelight. 'Are you saying I'm the first man who ever kissed you?'

'*Sí*. That ees true.'

'So, you are suddenly in love and come running to find me?'

'*Sí*, that is true, too. What is wrong, Mike? Don' you wan' me?'

He sighed and took another bite of the sausage. 'It ain't as easy as that, Rosa.'

'Why not easy? What you say, Mike? You don' love me?'

'Look, honey,' he put an arm around her, hugging her into him. 'Sure, when I looked into them eyes of yourn you hit me outa the blue. But you're just a gal, Rosa. I'm nearly thirty. I've been around. I gotta lot of wild cat in me. I don't want to hurt you, honey.'

'Mike, you not married, are you?'

'Nope, I ain't branded.' He glanced at her, uneasily. 'Not yet.'

'Oh,' she sang out, snuggling into him, 'I know you must have had other romances, but is in past. Ees you and me now.'

Morgan grinned ruefully. 'Well, I admit I'm travelling with a few old saddle-sores. But it ain't that. I got a responsibility to my partner, Pop Clancy, to our company, to the railroad we're building. Don Emilio, your father, ain't gonna like this. We gotta keep him sweet or he could withdraw his backing, leave us high and dry.'

'Oh, he is not that bad. He would not do that.'

'I ain't so sure.'

Rosa pulled away from him, angrily. 'You saying you don' wan' me, you don' wan' to marry me?'

'Marry you?' He couldn't help sounding like a scalded cat. 'One kiss don't mean we got to get married, gal. Not in Texas it don't.'

He was so unnerved by her anger that he did burn himself as he reached for the coffee-pot. 'Ouch!'

Rosa had sprung to her feet, pulling on her hat. 'I am fool. I make mistake. I theenk you love me. But you do not. To you I am just like cabaret girl. I must go.'

'Don't be so stupid. So naïve.' He

jumped up to catch hold of her, and she seemed to dissolve into tears in his arms. 'Come on, honey, quit that.' He was kissing her hair, her tear-wet eyes. 'Of course I love you,' he soothed, 'but we gotta take our time, do this right.'

'Yes,' she whispered. 'You are right, Mike. It would be good if my father give me away in church. It will please him for me to have a full white wedding in front of our friends, the whole of town.'

Church? Wedding? What was it with Mexican gals? he wondered. It seemed to be the main thing on their mind. But maybe it was time he thought of settling down. 'OK,' he said, 'we'll talk about that. But soon as the moon's fit to rise I'm gonna take you home. Your father must be worried sick.'

He settled her down by the fire and said, 'I'd better go make sure that murdering sonuvabitch ain't wriggled outa his bonds. Be back in a minute.'

He was greeted by a caustic, mocking laugh when he reached his prisoner.

'You an' the li'l girlie havin' a high ol' time up in the trees by the sound of it. You finished with her? What's she like, tasty?'

Morgan clenched his fist to take a punch at him, but held himself back. 'If you didn't have that busted shoulder I'd smash your dirty mouth in.'

'Aw, don't play holy joe with me, pal. You can tell me. Did she . . . ?' Pike leered at him as Morgan struck a match. He started making crudely obscene comments. 'Don't worry, I won't tell her daddy.'

'Shuddup. Don't push me too far.' Morgan tested the ropes for tightness. 'I'm taking you back to town. They'll patch you up ready for your hanging.'

'You think? Ever since I been old enough to suck whiskey from a jug I been one jump ahead of a noose. They ain't gonna stretch my neck just yet. Didn't you hear? They don't hang gringos down here nowadays. Not if they're working on the railroad. It gives the *rurales* too much paper work. You

102

think they give a shit about some *vaquero* and a coupla Chinks who've been killed? Don't make me laugh, pal.'

Morgan knew it was true. Porfirio Diaz wanted to encourage foreign investment. He had made railroad companies gifts of land, exempted them from Mexican laws and taxes. Morgan's own company was a beneficiary.

'Hey,' Pike called mockingly, as Morgan stamped away. 'Is this how you treat a prisoner? I got rights. How about some of that grub and coffee you two been hogging? The smell is torturing me. Come on, be a white man.'

Morgan turned and called back through the darkness, 'I ain't waitering to you, mister. To tell the truth I been wonderin' if it might be best to put a bullet in ya. You're too much of a damn troublemaker.'

'Aw, come on,' Pike sang out, 'or I'll snitch to Don Emilio. He won't like what you been doin' to his li'l girlie.'

'All I'm gonna give you is some

water, enough to keep you alive.' Morgan took his wooden canteen from the mule's saddlehorn, caught hold of Pike by the scruff of his neck, jerking his head back, and jammed the spout of the water-bottle down his throat.

'There,' he growled, as the killer choked and spluttered. 'Tell me whenever you're thirsty.'

★ ★ ★

Don Emilio was rumbling with rage inside like a volcano about to blow its top. But he had to maintain an icy-cool face as, that afternoon, he presided over the bullfight at Santa Rosa. Guest of honour was the state governor, Don Louis de Vasconcelos, with his lady and entourage from the capital, who were gathered around Don Emilio in the main box, so he was obliged to make polite small talk.

'Where's Rosa?' Don Louis had enquired and Terrazos was forced to make excuses, to lie that she had a headache and had begged leave not to attend.

Don Emilio was one of only seventeen people in the state who owned between them ninety per cent of its total area. Not an unusual pattern, and Don Louis had grabbed a major share of it. But these were perilous times and both Vasconcelos and Terrazos were forced to show strong loyalty to the Diaz regime if they were to retain their places in the pyramid of power.

'Where is Rosa?' was a question Don Emilio had demanded when he arose from a short siesta that day. 'What? She has gone riding? You fool,' he had shouted at the groom. 'Why did you not report this to me? Who allowed her out of the main gate? I will have his hide for this.'

Don Emilio generally enjoyed the spectacle and skill of a fight, but this one was torture not only for the bulls, but for him. He had left orders that when his daughter returned from her ride she should attend the reception he was giving at his town house for the governor.

He seethed with anger when there was no sign of her. 'What is the matter with her these days?' he debated with Ferdinand in a lowered voice as wine and refreshments were passed around. 'Rosa was such a docile girl. We were always so close. But now she deliberately flouts my authority. It was her duty to be here.'

'I don't like it, sir. She was exceeding brusque towards me at the ball last night,' Lopez replied in his guttural tone of voice. 'I fear she may be infatuated with that *Americano*.'

'God forbid!' A chill dread came over Don Emiliano. 'Ride out to the hacienda. Find out what she is playing at.'

Ferdinand Lopez patted the new, slimline automatic pistol in the inside pocket of his jacket, and his eyes narrowed as he hissed, 'Maybe the best way is to get rid of him?'

Don Emiliano pursed his lips, considering this. 'I'm not sure we need such drastic action — just yet. The finger of suspicion would be pointed our way. I don't want to completely alienate her. I am thinking of sending her to Europe to finish her education. It would get him out of her system.'

'He could have an accident.'

'No, Ferdinand. Go, hurry.'

Don Emilio tried to hide his discomfiture and put the guests at ease. Most of them were close friends of his own status in society. But he could not hide his agitation when Lopez returned at the gallop to report that Rosa had not been seen since riding away over the plain followed by the *vaquero*, Jorge.

'Why didn't the others go after her?'

'They didn't think it necessary. They thought Jorge would look after her.'

'Is that what they call protection? The times I have warned them to watch out for her,' Don Emilio raged. 'I must go search for her, Ferdinand. You stay and attend to the governor.'

But Vasconcelos was as concerned as

everyone at the news. 'She is in danger. We have had reports of bandits roaming the hills. No, don't protest, take Lopez with you, and ten of my *rurales*. We will return to the capital. You have my permission to take whatever action you consider necessary. Keep me informed.'

A good many of the male guests were already attired in traditional riding-outfits, tight-fitting, embroidered suits and sombreros for the fiesta, and were keen to join the posse that was being formed. Don Emilio hurriedly opened his armoury and equipped them all with guns and ammunition.

The horsemen clattered out of town to the hacienda and on across the plain, spreading out to search three different routes. 'We will meet up at the edge of the plateau, by the mule trail,' Terrazos shouted.

By the time they reached it the sun had melted away behind the rim, dusk had fallen fast and Don Emilio disconsolately debated the advisability of proceeding further with the horses across the dangerously rocky terrain.

'Look,' Lopez cried, pointing to a spot about a mile away up among the pine-trees. 'Somebody's got a fire going.'

'Come on.' Don Emilio raced away again, but called a halt at the foot of the ravine, saying they should dismount and proceed on foot, with caution. 'Try to maintain silence,' he lectured the pistol-happy *rurales*. 'We must not put my daughter in danger. Do not shoot unless I give the order. Try to curb your natural enthusiasm for killing.'

Some of the guests exchanged grins. Don Emilio was well-known for his brand of supercilious sarcasm. Most were enjoying the excitement of the outing and hoping for action. But they set off walking in Indian file up the ravine.

The whinny of a horse stopped Don Emilio in his tracks. There were three of them, and a mule, tethered in the darkness, the white hide and mane of Blaze most visible. 'That's Rosa's horse,' her father whispered, cocking his diamond-studded revolver and creeping forward. He nearly stumbled over two bodies and a man roped to a tree.

'Hey,' Hank croaked, hearing the sound of their spurs and peering at their vague shapes. 'Don't fire. I ain't armed.'

'Who are you?' Don Emilio demanded as matches were struck revealing their faces in the glow. 'What is going on?'

'You're Don Emilio, aincha?' Hank crowed, recognizing him. 'You'd be surprised, pal, what that li'l daughter of yourn is up to.' He nodded up towards the fire. 'Gor swizzle! I been listening to 'em giggling and making merry. God knows how many times that horny bastard's given it to her.'

The blood drained from Don Emilio's face as he glanced at Lopez. 'I will handle this, gentlemen. Wait for me.'

But his company were too curious to obey and followed at his heels as he crept up the slope.

* * *

The long rides both had had that day must have exhausted them for Mike Morgan and Rosa had drifted asleep by the fire as they waited for the moon to rise. He had thrown his coat around her shoulders to protect her from the chill night air of the high mountains. They had lain back on his soogans beside the fire and she had naturally curled her body into him as he held her protectively in his arms. And that was how they were found.

'Aw, no,' he groaned, as he suddenly awoke and became aware of the circle of *rurales* and Mexican gentlemen staring at him from the other side of the fire, all with rifles or revolvers pointed threateningly at him. There was no point in going for his S & W. 'This don't look good, do it?'

For moments Don Emilio was rapt in scandalized silence as he took in the sight of his daughter lying in the big American's arms. He noticed that one of his hands was reclining close to her bodice, a bodice that had been ripped away to reveal a glimpse of her pale, bare breasts.

Suddenly Rosa awoke, met his eyes and understood his shocked condemnation. She sat up, trying to pull her torn blouse together, to cover herself before the men's prying gaze. She looked from one face to another, friends of her father whom she recognized, and there was little doubt what they were thinking.

'It was the other man did this,' she protested. 'He attacked me. Mike saved my life.'

'Yes,' her father replied, snidely, 'but did he save your virtue? It does not appear so.'

'Don't be stupid,' Morgan said, getting to his feet. 'Your *vaquero*, Jorge, killed one of them two thugs. That other fella tied up down there shot Jorge. So I disarmed him. You can take him back for his trial.'

'It's you we are taking back. Cuff

him, you men,' Don Emilio ordered. 'Take his guns. Don't let him out of your sight.'

'Hey, what's all this about?' Morgan tried to struggle as two of the *rurales* held him and manacled his wrists in front of him. 'There ain't no need for this. I was just about to bring her home.'

'Leave him alone,' Rosa cried. 'This is crazy.' But she knew she was condemned in their eyes.

'You had best stay quiet, daughter,' Don Emilio snapped. 'I am just ensuring that your, what should I call him — friend? does not try to run away.'

7

It was dawn by the time Don Emilio and his wealthy gentlemen friends, attended by a squad of the hated *rurales* in their scarlet capes and sombreros, wheeled their horses towards the hacienda. The *peons* who lived in the *jacals* clustered around the walls were already making their way out to the allotments and orchards by the river. Men doffed their straw-hats and bowed low, their women curtsied, as the armed horsemen went clattering by. *Gapuchines* they called them — the wearers of spurs. For three centuries the people had been under their heel. There had been brief years of freedom and promise led by the beloved Benito Juárez. But now the 'spur-wearers' were back in power and had been for the past twenty years.

'They had two *Americanos* in manacles,' one muttered. 'What is going on?'

'I don't know,' his friend replied, 'but did you see Señorita Rosa? She looked very pale. It is said she has been away all night.'

Morgan was pulled unceremoniously from his mule and escorted by two armed men to a small room of the house, where his manacles were removed and he was left on his own, the door firmly bolted. 'What'n hell's going on?' he wondered.

After kicking his heels for an hour or so, he was collected by two *vaqueros*, armed with shotguns, and led along an echoing corridor to a gloomy chapel. The gentry, in their festive costume, were standing in silence awaiting him. At the end of an aisle parting their ranks he saw Rosa in a dress of shiny grey crêpe-de-Chine, a headdress and veil, standing beside her father. 'Forward.' One of the *vaqueros* nudged him with his shotgun and, somewhat reluctantly, Mike Morgan approached the ornate altar.

Before he could make any objection

— he was dumbfounded, what could he say? — the family priest had stepped forward with his Bible, taking Rosa's hand to join it with the tall Texan's, and was gabbling out a stream of Latin. Rosa parted her veil and stared at him with sadness, almost pleading: 'He is asking if you will take me as your wife?'

Morgan met her dark, lustrous eyes and growled, 'Yeah, I guess so. Why not?' The priest repeated his name and the question insistently, and there was another nudge of the shotgun. '*Sí*,' he said loudly, in Spanish. 'I do.'

There was no rejoicing, no drinks party. It was a shameful, solemn occasion. The *vaqueros* escorted him back to the great hallway of the house where they waited by the big oak door. Presently Don Emilio approached and said, 'Rosa will be down in a minute or two. She is packing a few personal belongings. She can take the stallion. It was a gift to her. I hope you're pleased with your night's work.'

'What do you mean?'

'Ha! Don't play the innocent. You thought you could marry into my money. Bad luck. She will have no dowry. I am cutting her off without a peso. You both disgust me.'

'Look, mister. I don't care who you are.' Morgan grabbed him by his cravat and raised his clenched fist. 'Take that back or I'll smash your words down your throat.'

'Keep your hands off me, you oaf.' Don Emilio cried, as the *vaqueros* jumped to intervene.

Relenting, Morgan released the *haciendado* as he saw Rosa approaching. She was still in the shiny grey dress of crêpe-de-Chine, carrying a small bundle under her arm wrapped in a *serape*. Her grandmother, Doña Cleminio, in her ornate dress and diamonds, had come from a side room and stood staring with an air of haughty disdain, coldly silent as the girl stepped by.

'Father,' Rosa pleaded, 'won't you at least give us your blessing.'

Don Emilio's face registered no

emotion. 'You have disgraced your family, your mother's memory, Rosa. You have chosen your own path. Go with him.'

'Come on,' Morgan gritted out, putting an arm around her. 'Let's git outa here.'

As the door was opened for them he turned and asked, 'How about the railroad, our contract? Is that still on?'

'If you reach Matarote first your company will receive payment according to the contract,' Don Emilio quietly replied. 'But somehow I doubt you will.'

Morgan stood and eyed him for a few seconds, then shrugged and joined Rosa outside in the courtyard. 'I'm gonna make him eat those words,' he vowed. 'Where's that damn mule?'

★ ★ ★

When he asked for their best room in the Hotel Real the manager stared at them like a frightened stoat. 'Señorita

118

Terrazos! What?' he stuttered. 'You cannot.'

'She's Mrs Morgan now, pal. Pass us the pen to sign in. How much fer one night?' He took a roll of greenbacks from his back pocket. 'I'll pay in dollars. OK?'

When the manager took her bundle and started to lead her up the stairs, Morgan called, 'I need a beer, honey. I'll see ya in a while.'

Damn Mexico. Even the beer didn't taste like beer. More like dog's piss. He spat it out. 'Hey, you got any mescal? Gimme a bottle.'

He was seething with suppressed anger. At the back of his mind he knew he shouldn't drink. It would just as likely make matters worse. But, what the hell? He took a slug of the fiery liquor from the neck. 'Christ!' He studied the label. 'What the hell do they put in this stuff?'

He went out and sat on the veranda, tried to calm down. The fiesta was over, the cobbled street outside was quiet apart from the wail of a wandering flower-seller. 'They sure suckered me,' he muttered to himself. 'Who'da thought it? One minute I'm free as a bird. The next, well, oh, I dunno, she's OK, a sweet kid, but I would've liked the chance to think about it first.'

Pop Clancy, Rowdy and the rest of the gang had by now boarded their locomotive and, with its trucks, it was headed back up the track to the tunnel. He would have a twenty mile ride up the mountainside on the mule to join them. Well, he was entitled to a day off for his honeymoon. He took another slug from the bottle. And another . . .

★   ★   ★

The chief *rurale* sat behind his desk and examined Hank Pike's belongings, his revolver, ammunition, lottery tickets, whorehouse tokens, marlin spike, string and oddments from his pockets including a billfold containing fifty-five dollars and 200 pesos in notes. He poked a stubby, grubby finger at a variety of silver peso and quarter coins, scratched at his unshaven jaw and remarked, 'You carry a lot of cash, *hombre*.'

Pike stood handcuffed before him and snarled, 'Thar's more where that come from.'

His meaningful remark entered the consciousness of the big-jawed *rurale*, who for a long while thought about Don Emilio's words: 'This man dared to touch my daughter. He must be shot. See to it.' When a man of his standing spoke thus it was generally not ignored. But . . .

'All that cash gotta be accounted fer and sent to my next-of-kin back in Missouri.'

'Yes,' the *jefe* sighed, 'a gringo corpse give me much trouble.' He picked up his quill, dipped it in ink, glanced at the two scruffy guards and snapped, 'You can go. I wish to interrogate the prisoner on my own.'

When they had gone, slamming the office door of the adobe jail, Pike drawled, 'Wise move, pal. There's a hundred bucks more for you next time I ride this way.'

The police chief stood, smirked, as he raked the cash to him, took his keys, and unmanacled Hank's proferred wrists. 'I will hold you to that promise, señor. You are free to go. Try not to kill any more of Don Emilio's men.'

Pike grinned tobacco-blackened teeth, holstered his revolver, and swaggered out, tugging his hat over his brow.

'If Don Emilio asks I will tell him it was the order of high-ups,' the *jefe* muttered. 'We have to be good to the gringos and they are good to us.'

★ ★ ★

Morgan had to admit his mind had begun to waver a bit, and his words were a tad slurred when he climbed the rickety hotel stairs to find Rosa.

'Jeez, I'm whacked,' he announced as he pushed into the darkened room. 'Ain't had no shut-eye since the night before last. Guess it's time for a siesta.'

The curtains were drawn and she was face down on the bed, still in the shiny grey dress. He unbuckled his gunbelt and slung it over the brass bedhead. He perched his hat on the knob and eased off his boots and leather chaps. Suddenly he realized her shoulders were shaking as she stifled a sob.

'Hey, come on, sweetheart,' he said, stroking her back. 'It ain't the end of the world.'

'You're angry,' she whispered. 'You think I tricked you. It OK. I geev you divorce.'

'Divorce? Ain't that against your religion?' He ran fingers through her mass of black hair. 'No, what's done's done. We're wed now, gal, for better or worse. So, we better git on with it.' He pulled her around to face him and tried to kiss her tears away, but she tensed and turned her head to one side.

'What do you mean?' she hissed. 'Are you drunk?'

'Look, I'll give it ya straight down the

gun-barrel. In Texas we like to work hard and play hard. And I figure a man's wedding-day is a day for play.'

He caught hold of one of her thighs and tried to hook it around his waist as he fell on top of her but she froze as cold as a corpse. 'Please, don't,' she begged. 'No, I don' wan' to.'

'Hm?' He studied her, quizzically. 'It's gonna be like that, is it?' He wanted to be gentle with her, to soothe her, but she was not having any, resisting his every move. Suddenly he was angry again. Sometimes a man had to get into the saddle and do what a man had to do.

'Stop, please, you're hurting me!' she cried out as the bed rattled against the wall, but there was no way he was going to cease until he was done.

To make matters worse she started sobbing again, curled up by his side as he lay back and caught his breath afterwards. 'I never knew it ees like that,' she whispered. 'What a man ees like. Nobody ever tol' me. I'm sorry.'

'You're all right. You gotta relax, Rosa,' he said, stroking her hair, saddened and somewhat ashamed. 'You gotta loosen up. You're on too tight a rein. You'll see. It'll be OK.'

They slept for a couple of hours, entwined together, but somehow apart. When he woke he listened to noises out in the street and rolled a cigarette. 'I been thinkin',' he told her. 'First light of dawn I'll head up into the mountains to join the boys. I'll pay for you to stay here in the hotel while I'm away.'

She was silent for a bit and then said, 'You don' wan' me with you, is that it?'

'No, that ain't it. It's hard work, man's work up there. No place for a gal. I'll be slogging away all hours God makes. We gotta git that railroad finished on time. We sleep in tents, for Christ's sake. It's no place for you. You ain't used to roughing it. It's best you stay here.'

'You don' love me. To you it was just a game.'

Morgan sighed. 'Wimmin! You allus

125

got to play that card.' He jammed his hat on his head, swung his legs from the bed, and sought his boots. 'Of course I love ya.'

'So.' She turned to him on one elbow, catching his arm. 'Take me with you. Prove you do. I won' get in the way.'

'OK, you win. I'm starvin' hungry. Let's go see what vittles they can rustle up in this joint.'

* * *

Pike cursed his mustang, gasping from a stab of pain from the wound in his right shoulder, kneeing the bronco in the gut, trying to jerk the saddle girth tight with his left hand. 'Stay still, you ornery critter!'

'Here, let me give you a hand, señor.' A guttural voice rasped out. 'I am glad to see they have let you free.'

Pike glanced at the dandified Mexican in his white suit and ornate boots who had stepped into the stable yard behind the jailhouse and had grabbed hold of the mustang's head. 'I don't need no help, pal,' he snarled. 'I take care of things on my own.'

'So, I see.' Fernando Lopez flashed his shark's teeth. 'You have escaped your appointment with the firing-squad, huh?'

'Yeah,' Hank growled. 'I know how thangs are done in this stinkin' country.'

'That wound must be giving you hell.'

'It ain't so bad. Bullet went clean through the flesh. It'll be OK in a week or so.' The tall American completed his harnessing. 'So, what's a dude like you want here, or need I ask?'

Lopez gave a deep laugh. 'I've just been passing the time of day with a friend of yours and his new bride. Neither look very happy.'

'Morgan? He's married the bitch?'

'*Sí*, it was a case of having to, although I think Don Emilio acted with foolish haste. But he is a proud man. That's the way it is in Mexico. We have a great misguided sense of honour.'

Pike jerked the mustang's head around. 'So what's it got to do with you, mister?'

'Me?' Lopez chuckled hoarsely again. 'I am the jilted party. She is — she *was* my girl until your interfering Texan friend came along.'

'I see.' Hank studied him, savouring this information. 'So you were after moving into Don Emilio's favour, gittin' your paw into his money-bags?'

'You put it crudely, my friend.' Lopez looked around, furtively, to make sure they were not overheard. '*Sí*, in my sadness I would not grieve if an accident befell Rosa's husband.'

'That could be arranged. Where is he?'

'Taking breakfast with his beloved in the hotel.'

'Waal, I ain't up to facing him out right now.' Hank Pike flexed the fingers of his right hand. 'It'll be a coupla weeks 'fore I get my shooting prowess back with a sixgun. So how much would this accident be worth to you?'

Lopez laughed in his savage way. 'I am not a rich man, *señor*. Not yet, at least. It might be different if Rosa were free to marry again. She might be persuaded the next time to marry the man her father has chosen for her.'

'Yeah, OK, so how much?'

Ferdinand Lopez lowered his voice. 'They are about to leave to ride up along the railroad track to join the rest of the crew. If they did not get there I would be happy to part with, say, five hundred dollars.'

'Yeah? But I'm broke. That li'l rat of a *rurale* chief cleaned me out. So, I'll need a downpayment.'

Ferdinand looked slant-eyed about him again, and pulled a hundred dollars in bills from his back pocket. 'Surely this should make your task more appetizing?'

Pike patted his Spencer carbine in the saddle boot. 'Consider it done.' He snaffled the cash, then with some difficulty swung into the saddle. 'To tell the truth, pal, it will be a pleasure.'

129

8

They had followed the rail track for fifteen miles and entered an area of steep-sided ravines, solid rock through which the route had been blasted. Where a stream tumbled down from the mountainside water had been channelled into a big tank to service the locomotive. A stack of logs for fuel had been left in readiness.

'We'll take a rest,' Morgan said, jumping from the mule and offering a hand to Rosa to help her step down from the white stallion. He caught her and held her in his arms for a few moments, but she broke away to take Blaze's reins to lead him to water.

There was already a tension between them and as he knelt to build a small fire for their coffee-pot he wished he had insisted she stay in town. 'This ain't a good start to married life,' he muttered.

Indian voices distracted him and he looked up to see a herd of pigs being driven down the track. Grunting, curly tails waggling happily, they had been wandering for months in the hills eating acorns, juniper berries and grass. The weather-beaten face of the swineherd creased into a grin as he greeted them in an incomprehensible dialect, the boy with him watching warily as the pigs trotted to the stream to slake their thirsts.

Morgan offered them coffee and tobacco and tried to converse with them, mostly by sign language. 'Seems like they're taking the pigs into market,' he said.

Rosa sat in silence as the Indians peered at her, curiously. Not in the best of moods, she was sore, both in body and mind. She had been shocked by the rough, crude, drunken manner her husband had assumed to make love, as if as a man it was his right. She had been so protected, cosseted and kow-towed to by servants and *peons* all her life that she had never faced up to the hard facts of the sexually physical. How could she have remained so innocent, so naïve, so absurd?

'I have a lot of adjusting to do,' she told herself.

★   ★   ★

It was the perfect spot for a bushwhacker. The north side of the ravine had been dynamited and hacked away sheer to a clifftop and Morgan and his companions were unaware that Hank Pike had reached it and was peering over the rim. 'Aw, how cosy,' he sneered as he looked down at them 200 feet below, sipping coffee and smoking cigarettes. 'Just hold it right there a second, folks.'

The seven-shot Spencer was set steady between the V-gap of two rocks. It would be easy enough to fire with his left hand, hardly having to use his right arm. He lay flat, taking first pressure on the trigger, lining up the sights on

Morgan's back. 'So long, sucker!'

But as he fired the Texan leaned to one side to retrieve the coffee-pot for a refill and the bullet tore through his shirt-sleeve. Instead of him, it was a pig who squealed with pain and rolled towards the rails, kicking as it pumped blood.

'Down!' Morgan yelled, hurling himself at Rosa, knocking her flying off her log seat to hit the ground. He dragged her unceremoniously up onto her knees, and scrambled into the lee of the cliffside, dragging her with him.

'Damn him!' Hank shouted in desperation. It was by no means easy to lever another slug into the Spencer with his gammy arm. He had thought to kill Morgan with the first bullet. He eventually had another ready but then he had to abandon the support of the two rocks and wriggle closer to the edge to aim at them. 'There they are,' he gritted out and let loose the lead. 'Shee-it!'

He cursed, for at that moment

Morgan had commanded Rosa to keep her head down and had made a dash for his mule. The bullet sparked flints from the rocks where a second before he had been crouched.

It was Pike's turn to duck back as Morgan pulled the Winchester from his bedroll and without hesitation sent a non-stop volley of six streaking and whining past his head. Pike held onto his Stetson and tried to wriggle back to safety.

'I don't believe it!' Pike had rolled onto his back to lever another bullet into the breech, but the Spencer jammed. No amount of fiddling, knocking the mechanism against the rock would release it. 'It ain't my day. I'm gittin' outa here.'

Down below Morgan waited warily to get a glimpse of the backshooter, but the only assault came from a small rock hurled derisively by Pike as he made his escape, which bounced harmlessly onto the rails.

'I think he's gawn,' Mike shouted

after a while. 'Unless I got him, which I doubt.'

But he kept a wary eye on the top of the cliff as the Indian in his ragged clothes gabbled at him, pointing to the dead pig. 'All right, I'll pay fer it if you gut it,' Morgan shouted, back to using sign language again. 'We could do with some fresh meat.'

'Who was it?' Rosa asked, obviously shaken.

'Who do you think? That fella whose acquaintance you made the night before last,' he grunted. 'At least that's my opinion. I didn't get a look at him, but who else would it be?'

'I don't know,' she said, and shuddered. 'Why? What is it for, all this killing?'

He tied the butchered pig's carcass onto the back of his saddle and swung aboard without helping her on to the stallion. 'I'm gonna leave you to figure that out for yourself.'

★ ★ ★

135

Pop Clancy's jaw dropped when he saw them ride in. He pointed at the girl. 'What's she doing here?'

'Hey, Señorita Terrazos, you look a picture,' Rowdy cried. 'But this ain't no place for a lady.'

'What are you trying to do?' Clancy squawked. 'Ruin us all? I ought to punch you on the jaw. What's Don Emilio — '

'Meet the wife.' Morgan cut him short as he climbed down.

'What?' Clancy's Adam's apple bounced with alarm in his scrawny throat. 'You married her? Have you really gone loco?'

'I didn't have much choice,' the Texan drawled. 'Not with a shotgun in my back.'

Rosa heard the remark and winced. 'My father, he get the wrong idea. But, yes, we are married now.'

'Whoo-hoo!' Rowdy yelped, slapping his friend on the back. 'I never thought to see Mad Mike Morgan tamed.'

'Here.' Morgan threw the pig hard at him. 'Roast pork on the menu tonight.

No point in asking Rosa to cook it. She ain't the domesticated sort.'

The girl could not be unaware of the sarcastic bitterness of his tone. 'I will do my share,' she fired back. 'Just show me how.'

'That's a good gal, Rosa,' Rowdy exclaimed. 'I'll teach ya how to spit it, turn it, baste it. You'll soon larn.'

'Even though she's never done a hand's stir all her life,' Pop muttered, shaking his head. 'You've really put us in a fix now, Mike. I thought things were bad enough.'

'Why, what's wrong?'

Pop nodded towards the tunnel entrance blocked by rubble. 'Wang's dead. Either he was trying to do some tunnelling on his own. Or somebody brought it all down on his head. We're back to where we started.'

Morgan digested these facts, looking around at the disconsolate *peons* and the Chinese who had arrived, awaiting orders to start work. 'All right, boys. This looks bad, I know. But they ain't gonna stop us. We won't go through the mountain. We'll go around the side. Any of ya know anythang about constructing bridges? No? Waal, we're all gonna have to learn. Come on, let's get organized. We ain't got time to hang around.'

★   ★   ★

In the early morning Ferdinand Lopez, in his Panama hat, white-linen suit and silk cravat, travelled on the new railroad built by the Clancy-Morgan company from Santa Rosa down to the fetid, unhealthy coastal strip. As the train rattled rhythmically along the track in the winding descent from the high mountain wall, he toyed with his new slide-automatic pistol. It had a slim, potent look, the first of its kind, a revolutionary design, obtained in the pre-production stage from Germany. In block sans-serif style on its side was the legend '1896 **Waffenfabrik Mauser AG Obendorf**'. Lopez took a few shots out of the open window at a flock of wild turkey by the side of the track, making them scatter in a shower of feathers.

'What a beauty!' He grinned at a lady, the only other passenger, and tucked the weapon snugly back into the inside pocket of his suit. 'This is the future.'

Paul Mauser had been making weaponry for the past thirty years and the American companies had nothing comparable. He settled back on the hard, slatted seat and watched the female across the aisle. In a long skirt and modest blouse, deep-bosomed, with a straw-hat perched on her abundant black hair, her brown complexion was masked by a thick layer of purple powder and rouge. She seemed to have a preference for carmine nails. Ferdinand flashed his teeth and moved across to squeeze beside her. The gold weding-band on her finger and her obvious middle-class air did not deter him. Any woman was fair game when

Lopez was aroused. Maybe he could make her before they reached the next halt?

He looked even more smugly satisfied when he jumped from the train at Puerto, a busy harbour and fishing-port. He was officially on business for Don Emilio, sent to find out what had happened to the iron rails and other supplies. Yes, the cargo had arrived and was being unloaded that day. 'Hold on to it until you get further orders,' he said.

Lopez decided to board a train on the railroad that hugged the coast and headed south to the estuary of the river where an alternative shipment port was being constructed. At the headquarters of the California & Gulf company he was introduced to the boss man, a dark-jowled character, Al Stevens, who sprawled at an overloaded desk.

'Yeah,' he drawled, 'how can I help ya? I'm a busy man. Spit it out.'

'It's a question of how can I help you,' Lopez replied in his guttural accent.

'You say you're Don Emilio's right-hand man. But he's backing the Clancy outfit.'

'Maybe I would prefer the C and G to get to the mines first. I've already done a deal with your man Pike to get rid of Clancy's partner.'

'Morgan? That slime-bucket. He had the nerve to steal all my coolies. It was a hold-up. I've had to send to San Francisco to get some more shipped down. You Mexicans are too damn slow and idle to get things done. You can't beat Chinese. The best railroad workers in the world.'

Lopez was not an uneducated man and pointed out that perhaps Mexico's maize-based culture might be the cause of the *peons*' lassitude. 'They are not lazy, just undernourished. If you fed them some protein, some of your beef, it might help.'

'Ya, a good excuse. How come the Chinks manage on a bowl of rice? As for that *hombre* Pike, he ain't produced much in the way of results so far.' Al

141

got up and closed the office door. 'Whadda ya mean? You serious about getting rid of Morgan?'

'Mister,' Lopez growled, 'I've never been more serious in my life. I could help you in other ways, too.'

'Oh, yeah. Such as?'

Lopez sighed and shrugged. '*Señor*, I am not paid well by Don Emilio — '

'Huh? Like that, is it? How much do you want?'

'There is a consignment of rails, cement, tools, waiting to be shipped up to Santa Rosa. For payment of a mere one thousand dollars I could arrange for them to be shipped to you instead.'

'You don't come cheap, do you?'

'On the contrary, you will be getting an excellent bargain,' Lopez said, and outlined the size of the cargo. 'I am doing you a big favour at not inconsiderable risk to my own position if this should get out.'

'Don't worry, it'll be kept hush-hush.' Al Stevens took a bottle from his drawer. 'I think we can do business, *amigo*. Any other ideas?'

'I can make sure you get the contract. But Morgan's a tough character. Perhaps you need to bring in a couple more hard men to support Pike.'

'I've already sent for a couple of guys. The best.' Al poured a couple of tots of whiskey. 'Here's to us, chum. The Clancy-Morgan outfit is as good as dead. So how do you want payment, pesos or dollars?'

Lopez grinned and tossed back the liquor. 'Dollars will suit me fine.'

★ ★ ★

'We gotta git finished 'fore the rains start,' Mike abruptly replied to Rosa when she complained that she hardly ever saw him, that he was pushing himself and the workers too hard. 'You don't understand.'

It was true that he was working like a madman, obsessed with reaching the mines another twenty miles ahead in the mountain range. If he was not supervising the Chinese grading the track around the edge of a precipice, he was down in a deep ravine, with Murphy wielding his club to urge the *peons* on, as they hacked down pines and began to construct a trestle-bridge. The Mexicans were used to resting through the hot afternoons but Morgan kept them going from dawn until dusk. He would only return to the camp at the end of the long summer evenings as the sun went down, and then he was too exhausted to do other than wolf down some food and tumble fast asleep on his separate cot in their small canvas tent.

'What's happened to that shipment of rails, the bags of cement we ordered, all the other stuff?' he asked Pop. 'We cain't lay track if we ain't got no rails.'

'Don Emilio says it's been delayed,' Pop replied. 'He's been told the cargo's failed to arrive in port.'

'Yeah?' Morgan spat out, angrily. 'It's time you went back to Puerto and found out what's going on. It sounds like a pack of lies to me, like Terrazos is holding it back, trying to ruin me like he threatened he would.'

'My father doesn't lie,' Rosa's voice rang out. 'He wouldn't do that to you.'

'Oh, no?' Mike glanced up, guiltily, for he had not realized his wife was close by. 'Well, I wouldn't put anything past that wily bird. Or that oily side-kick of his. Why don't you go and rustle up some grub? How much longer we got to wait?'

'It was ready two hours ago,' she replied, almost in tears. 'Now I have to heat it up again.'

Rosa had willingly taken on cooking for the Americans. The Irish boys and the Chinese looked after themselves, while a couple of Indian women camp-followers fed the Mexicans. But it was not something she had ever done before. The only cuisine she had any fondness for was the French-style introduced by the Empress Carlota, who was now in an asylum for the insane. Most Mexican food was fried and she was constantly exasperated as she tried to produce something tasty from their basic supplies. She had never washed a dish before in her life, let alone a greasy skillet, and was beginning to hate the stink of woodsmoke as she crouched over their fire. It would get in her eyes, linger in her clothes and hair. There was little chance to bathe and the sanitary arrangements were basic, indeed embarrassing, she being one of the few females amid this crowd of men. She watched the Indian women going about their tasks. Her lot was little different from theirs and it was tedious and hard. More and more she began to recall the crisp, laundered underwear, the silk stockings and dresses laid out for her by her maids, the flowers, the luxuries of her past life, with something akin to regret.

★ ★ ★

Pop Clancy returned on their locomotive to Santa Rosa the next day and cornered Don Emilio in his study at his town house.

'What's happened to the cargo of rails we've been waiting for for weeks?' he demanded.

'I have no idea. It's gone missing. As far as I know it hasn't yet arrived at Puerto. Or so I'm informed.'

'So, who give you this information?'

'Why, Ferdinand. I sent him down there to make enquiries only the other day.'

Pop was as angry as a disturbed hornet, leaning across the desk waggling his finger at the aloof *haciendado*. 'If you think you can sabotage our operation, mister, jest 'cause Mike Morgan's married to your precious daughter, you're biting off more than you can chew.'

'Why should I do that? I would advise you to calm down. I don't care to be threatened in my own house.'

'Well, you're gettin' me riled up,' Pop replied, almost dancing with agitation. 'Guess I'd better go down there and see what's happening for myself.'

'Yes, you do that.' Don Emilio gave a faint smile as he watched the diminutive Clancy turn away and head for the door. 'By the way,' he called, 'how is she?'

'She ain't so good. Morgan ain't one to enjoy being shotgunned into anything, least of all a wedding,' Pop called out. 'He's like a bear with a sore head and I figure he's taking it out on her.'

'Well, that rather serves her right, doesn't it? She's made her bed, so, as they say, she must lie in it.'

'Guess the life up there won't do her no harm. Should toughen her up. But she's a sweet, innocent gal and she don't deserve your treatment or his,' Pop sang out, before slamming the door and muttering, 'I gotta catch that train.'

* * *

Pop was still hopping mad when he reached Puerto, charging into the harbour clerk's office, demanding to see his files.

'Where's our cargo? Something funny's going on.' The clerk protested his ignorance as Clancy caught hold of him by his shirt front and shook him. 'Talk, you fat slug. I know a liar when I see one.' Like a strutting bantam Pop poked into cabinets, scattered papers in search of evidence, until the clerk called for assistance and Clancy was collared by two guards and tossed out of the building. 'Yeah,' he shouted through the window. 'I know what's going on. Somebody's put the frighteners on you, ain't they? I'm gonna complain to the president. You can't treat Americans like this.'

He was standing there seething when a dock-worker caught hold of his sleeve. 'You wan' know wha' happen to your cargo?' He was rubbing fore-finger and thumb together. 'I tell you.'

When Clancy had passed the appropriate bribe, the docker hissed, 'I help load it on other wagons. It go down coast. That man in flashy white suit, I hear him warn clerk to keep mouth shut, or else.'

'Was there an excessive smell of brilliantine about him?' Pop asked. 'Perfume?'

'*Sí*, there was, an' he wear big panama hat.'

'I mighta known. Ferdinand Lopez!'

9

'There's one sure way to stop 'em, that's to destroy their rolling-stock,' Pike drawled. 'Bridges can be rebuilt but if they ain't got a loco to put on it they won't be going nowhere.'

Al Stevens had come out on their own 'puffing Billy' from the estuary, dragging wagons carrying the rails, ties and cement that by rights ought to have gone to Santa Rosa. Even with Mexican workers their own track was proceeding by leaps and bounds although, admittedly, it was still following the flat river bank. However, once they started the gradual ascent they had every chance now of reaching the mines before Clancy and Morgan.

'That would certainly be the clincher, Pike, if you could do it without fouling up this time.'

'Aw, he's been lucky, thassall,' Pike

whined. 'We kin do it an' eliminate them two at the same time.'

'All I got to do is win this race and get the contract to satisfy the big boys back in California and their shareholders,' Al muttered. 'How we do it is up to you.'

'We'll be needing dynamite and fuses and spare ammunition.' Pike eyed the two hired guns Stevens had brought with him, who were busy getting their kicking and whinnying broncos off one of the cars. 'You think them two can handle it?'

'These boys come well recommended,' Al said as the two desperadoes sauntered across from the wagons to join them in the construction office. 'I'm certainly paying y'all enough. You got a free hand. No need to worry about the local *rurales*. They're on our side, too.'

He introduced George Baker, a sullen individual in a crumpled suit, bandanna and slouch hat, a sturdy Colt .45 holstered under his jacket. He had the dead eyes of a born killer.

The other was younger, more wiry and cocksure, attired *vaquero*-style in a loose orange shirt, leather waistcoat, flared trousers and spurs. His fair, greasy hair hung over his brow as he gave a caustic grin. 'The handle's Jones,' he said. 'You can call me Luke.'

Their names were obvious aliases, but what did it matter. Such men were easy enough to recruit among the scum of the border towns. 'What's that ye're packing?' Pike asked in his nasal whine.

Luke whipped out the nickel-plated .38 Sidewinder as soft as a whisper and levelled it at Pike with a fanatic smile. 'The best for the best,' he said. 'New swing-out cylinder, half-cock safety, staghorn grip, made of the finest Solingen steel.'

'Thirty-eight won't stop a man,' Pike muttered.

'This one will.' Luke spun it and slipped it back into his holster pig-stringed to his thiigh. 'You wanna try me?'

'Waal, I hope you shoot as fast as

your mouth, dude. Let's git started. We got a long three-day ride up into the mountains. Gotta take it easy 'cause of the altitude.

'Altitude don't bother me.' Luke grinned.

'If you git whoozy and fall off your hoss at eight thousand feet I might remind you of those words.' Pike scowled at Al. 'Ain't sure I can put up with this lippy li'l bastard fer too long.'

'Aw, you'll be OK,' Stevens said. 'I'm relying on you boys.'

★ ★ ★

Mike Morgan was balanced precariously a hundred feet up near the top of their trestle-bridge. They had spent weeks splitting pines, adzing them into shape, hammering them into the ground, fitting the jigsaw together, and now it was almost complete. The Chinaman, Ho, was swinging about, suspended from the end of a rope, guiding another trestle which was being craned down from the top. 'I got it,'

Mike yelled, slotting it into place. 'Steady now.' He began to hammer big iron bolts into its gouged-out holes as Ho held the top end diagonally in place. 'That's got it. Solid as a rock! Right, let's get the other one in.'

On the further side of the ravine Rowdy had gone on ahead, dynamiting a way through the rock and carving a path around a spur of the mountain. He was followed by an antlike procession of Irish, Chinese and Mexicans, shovelling away and tamping the grade down firmly. Each day they pushed forward another mile or so through the difficult terrain. They might not have any rails but they certainly had a track to lay them on.

While in Puerto Pop had cabled every possible acquaintance in the railroad industry who might be able to provide a cargo of rails and spikes by urgent dispatch. He did a jig in the street waving the cable by return from an old pal in Tucson, Arizona, promising to send the required materials by the coastal railroad down to Puerto. But it would take a matter of three weeks.

'It sure is cutting things fine because the rainy season could be on us in three weeks,' he said when he got back. 'It don't give us much time for track-laying.'

'Aw, that's the easy part,' Morgan replied as at last they relaxed about sundown after a long hard day. 'We can do it.'

Pop had brought back a couple of bottles of tequila for them, although he himself no longer imbibed. Rowdy and Mike had already taken a good bite out of their respective bottles, knocking it down by the neck.

Rowdy was in the middle of yarning about how he had got involved in a crooked card-game in Amarillo and had to get out of town fast before he got tarred and feathered.

'Why should that happen?' Rosa asked, perplexed.

Rowdy gave a howl of drunken

156

mirth. ''Cause I organized the damn game, that's why.'

Rosa shook her head. 'Why do men have to drink?' she asked. 'What good is it? It make no sense.'

'Aw, you don't understand,' Morgan slurred, and took another slug of the fiery stuff. 'You're too much of a puritan, Rosa. You oughta let your hair down now an' again.'

'All you do is make fools of yourselves.'

'So what? We'll be sober tomorrow, eh, Rowdy, ol' pal?'

'Did you know that the Toltec empire came to an end through excessive drinking? And the Aztecs only allowed people to get drunk when they were over seventy?'

'I sure cain't wait 'til then,' Rowdy cackled.

'It's all very well, but drunkenness is the curse of Mexico. Haven't you seen the Indian women feeding their six-month-old babies on pulque? What chance do those children have?'

'Jeez, I'm beginning to think you oughta be a missionary,' Morgan groaned, taking another swig. 'You're picking on the wrong guy, honey, 'cause I sure ain't going to join the League of Temperance. Ain't it time you saw to that stew?'

Men! They seemed to think a woman had no brains, was only there to be bed-warmer and bottle-washer. Indignant as she might be, Rosa thought it best not to get drawn in, and went outside to squat down by the fire to stir at the pot and sprinkle in a few more herbs she had collected from the mountainside as they worked.

'How much longer are we going to live like this?' she wondered. 'It is driving me crazy. Will this railroad ever be completed? Will we ever live a normal life, be happy again?'

She had begun to feel that Mike resented her being there, that he was trying to cut her out. It almost seemed as if he enjoyed rubbing her fine nose into the mud. She had planned to be more relaxed, more loving, but he hardly touched her these days, falling fast asleep on his separate bunk. The next thing she knew, before daylight he would be pulling his boots back on, groaning at his aching back and muttering about the work there was to be done. Sometimes Rosa wondered how much more she could take.

They had to duck their heads to get in and out of their own small tent, while their dining-area and 'office' was a canvas construction with a couple of trestle-tables and at least the luxury of folding chairs. On this particular night Rosa had managed to prepare a wild turkey that Mike had shot, and presented it in a richly-flavoured sauce. Only Rowdy commented that it was 'mighty fine'. Pop and Mike were so engrossed in their maps and plans by the light of a hurricane-lamp as to hardly notice what they ate.

'You ain't got those foundations of the bridge solid enough,' Pop whined. 'Come the rains — '

Mike cut him off, growling, 'It'll hold. We ain't got time an' we ain't got no cement, thanks to you-know-who.'

Suddenly Rosa snapped. She went out and fondled Blaze's head. She had thought it would be better to be up here in the mountains than to face the ridicule and whispers in the town, but now she was not so sure.

'He doesn't want us here,' she whispered to the stallion as she slipped the bridle over his ears, and tightened the saddle cinch. Mike was right. They were on opposite sides of a great divide. She left a note on his bunk in the tent: *Gone back to town.* She climbed on to Blaze and went trotting away down the track which was shimmering in the ghostly moonlight.

★ ★ ★

'Ain't you going after her?' Pop Clancy demanded in the morning.

'No, I ain't. I got a railroad to build.'

'What good's a railroad without rails?

160

Ease up, Mike, you're pushing the men too hard. You're cutting dangerous corners. It ain't like you. Why don't you slow down?'

'If you don't like the way I'm running this company you can get out,' Morgan growled. 'And that goes for anybody else.'

'Hey, pal,' Clancy stormed. 'I founded this company. I'm running it too. I'd like a bit of respect. You'd be nobody without my expertise.'

'Yeah, you founded it with my money. You were a hopeless drunk and I carried you — '

'You heartless bastard!' Pop clenched a fist, grabbing hold of Morgan's jacket and swinging a punch at him. 'What have you done to that girl? You don't care who you step on.'

Morgan blocked the blow and pushed the old man hard away, his eyes narrowed as Pop tripped and sprawled back in the dust by the rails. 'If you're so bothered about her you go find her. She couldn't take the pace. No doubt she'll be back in her daddy's arms by now.'

'You . . . ' Pop spluttered, helped to his feet by Murphy. 'You're as bad as him. You and your pride. OK, I'll go back to Santa Rosa, make sure she's all right.'

'You'll have to take the mule because I need the engine today. I'm putting in the last section of the bridge. When you're down there find out when those rails will arrive.'

'Not much hope of that,' Pop muttered, finding his hat and turning away. 'We'll be into the rains before then.'

'You shouldn't have done that,' Murphy protested as they watched him go. 'That man's been like a father to you, taught you everything you know.'

'If you don't like it, draw your pay and clear out, too.' Morgan eyed the Irishman fiercely as Murphy shook his shaggy head and glowered back like a cornered bull. 'No? Right, let's move.

We've got work to do.'

There was a flatbed truck holding an iron crane on the front of the locomotive. The engineer got up steam, shooting smoke from the tall stack into the clear mountain air and, with the final trestle section suspended from the crane, edged slowly forward into the centre of the bridge. Morgan stood hanging out from the flatbed trying to hold it steady. The labourers watching gave a rousing cheer as it slotted perfectly into place. 'Right, back off,' Mike shouted to the driver as Ho and his boys clambered along to bolt the trestle firmly into place.

The engine eased back to the edge of the ravine. 'Yeah,' Mike muttered, 'we got ourselves a bridge but we've run out of rails.' In fact, they had borrowed a section of rail from further back to extend out to the centre of the bridge. 'We better return those to where they came from 'fore there's an accident.' He turned to Rowdy. 'You still with me?'

The bearded Texan shrugged. 'I guess so.'

'Good. I want you to take the theodolite and survey right on ahead. See how much further we got to go to reach the mine.'

Rowdy grinned. 'Sure.'

By now it was gone midday, but Morgan allowed no let-up except for a break for water and a quick snack. 'Right,' he directed Ho, whom he had put in charge of the Chinese and *peons*, 'you go on over the ravine and carry on grading from as far as you've got. You might as well make camp up there tonight rather than march all them miles back. Tomorrow just carry on. Rowdy will peg out the route. There's only a couple more small *barrancas* to cross and the mine should be in sight.'

'OK, boss.' Ho cheerfully trudged off in his rags, sandals and Aladdin-style hat. 'C'm on, boys, chop chop!'

Morgan worked the rest of the day alongside Murphy and a couple of his boys putting finishing touches to the surface of the bridge. He peered down at the stream winding through the steep canyon walls below. 'That'll hold,' he muttered. 'It's got to.'

Murphy, sullen and silent, made no reply nor did he invite Mike to join them as they trudged back to their camp alongside the goods vans. They left the big locomotive and its front flat-loader right on the edge of the ravine where the rails came to an abrupt end.

'We got a bridge,' the driver said, 'but no way of getting us over.' He climbed into his cab to boil a kettle and cook a flapjack in his fire's embers.

'You better stay here tonight, Jock,' Morgan shouted. 'Keep an eye on things.'

His own tent seemed strangely lonesome as he crawled into it in the darkness. Maybe he had been a tad hard on Rosa, on Pop, he thought, bitterly. 'They just don't understand. If we don't get to that mine we'll be bankrupt.' All that effort would be wasted.

Morgan hugged his Winchester to him, pinched out the candle and in seconds, exhausted, mentally and physically, fell into the sleep of the dead.

10

'There's only two of 'em,' Pike gritted out, as they watched the men seated around their fire. 'Irish by the sound of their voices. Where's everybody else gotten to?'

'They've gawn,' young Luke Jones whined as he fondled his .38 Sidewinder.

'We can see they gawn,' George Baker growled, 'but where they gawn to?'

'Musta crossed the bridge and moved on up ahead.' Pike peered through the darkness illumined by a globe of pale moon. Beyond the men at the camp-fire the goods vans stretched forwards past several tents. The locomotive itself appeared to be perched on the edge of the ravine, its nose and a flatbed wagon in front poking just onto the mouth of the bridge. 'This suits us fine. Leave the hosses here. Don't shoot 'less you have to. We don't wanna rouse the others.'

He led the way stealthily along the far side of the cars, dropped down and slid beneath a wagon, wriggling towards the burly back of a curly-haired Irishman.

'Dat's a lovely blaze,' Murphy was saying, as Pike got to his feet and stuck his razor-sharp scalping-knife in his back.

His companion stared open-mouthed with horror as Murphy toppled forward. 'What the devil — ?' he began, but gasped, goggle-eyed, as Baker crept up from behind, slipped a wire noose over his head and jerked it tight.

'That's two down,' Pike hissed, listening. 'What's that?'

The sound of loud snoring emanated from a nearby pup tent. Morgan had instructed them to keep guard so they were taking three hours' sleep apiece, with three hours on watch. He had provided them with a shotgun and a heavy .303 Enfield rifle, all he could obtain in Santa Rosa where guns were banned to ordinary Mexicans. They had been carelessly left to one side.

'Get him,' Pike ordered, nodding at the tent.

'Gimme your knife,' Luke said, as he reached for the implement and ducked into the tent. There was not a sound as he slit the third man's throat. The snoring ceased. 'Right.' Luke grinned as he emerged. 'What next?'

Pike opened his shoulder-bag to show them sticks of dynamite, wires and fuses. 'We blow up the friggin' engine, that's what.'

'What about the bridge?'

'Nah, we ain't got time to clamber about in the dark. Our orders are to blow the train, then we git out. Come on.'

They passed the lean-to tent and several smaller tents that were in darkness and, they assumed, deserted, only checking a couple of them. They were in a hurry to reach the locomotive and get their task done. A glow from its firebox showed the way. Pike peered into the cab. The engineer was sitting with his feet up, dozing. He struggled awake as Pike climbed up to join him. 'Yes,' he stuttered, 'what do you want?'

Pike viciously buffaloed him with his revolver butt and the man fell back, K.O.'ed. 'Sweet dreams, pal.'

He dropped down the other side and peered into the steep depths of the ravine. 'This is gonna make one hell of a smash,' he called to the others. 'With any luck it'll take half the bridge with it.'

Pike had started wiring sticks of dynamite to the big wheels and rods of the locomotive when back in his tent Morgan awoke, gripping the Winchester to him. He had heard some sound in the night. Maybe it was just a coyote poking around. He was about to sink back asleep when men's voices carried to him on the mountain breeze. He swung off his cot and pulled on his boots. 'Who's that?' he muttered. 'What the hell's going on?'

He levered a slug into the breech of the Winchester as he peered up along the track. Two shadowy shapes of men were standing beside the engine. He was half-inclined to fire, but he wasn't sure who they were. Might they be the Irish poking about?

Instead, he put the Winchester aside, loosened his S & W in its holster and climbed up on to the top of one of the goods vans. It would give him a better view of proceedings. He carefully stepped along, leaping forward from one car roof to the next until he reached the tender of the engine. He lowered himself down on to piles of logs, and stepped forwards towards the cab. The two men had gone up ahead. He could hear them laughing harshly at another man who seemed to be underneath. Inside the cab the engineer was sprawled, unconscious. 'Christ!'

Morgan hung out from the cab by one hand, taking a shot at the two men, who were backing away as another tall figure scrambled from beneath the engine to join them. He fired again, but missed. They were running away as fast as they could, sending bullets whistling at his own head as they did so.

Suddenly the great iron locomotive heaved and shuddered as explosions thundered beneath it. Slowly, surely, it was tipped to one side and Morgan was thrown to the far side of the cab. It was too late to save the driver, or for that matter himself. He leapt out into black space as dynamite ripped and roared, the huge engine tumbled forwards, turned over in two somersault leaps on its nose, and crashed into the ravine, taking a cloud of dust, boulders, torn rails and struts of the bridge with it. Morgan's head hit a rock as he landed. Darkness closed over him . . .

★　★　★

After weeks living in the mountain wilderness it was like returning to a strange land to be back in Santa Rosa. People turned to stare at her as in her riding skirt, dusty boots and dirty, fire-scorched jacket she tethered the stallion outside the Hotel Real and went inside. As she sat in the dining-room sipping hot coffee with cream she was aware of the cook, the maids peeping through the bead curtain of the kitchen, of the other guests whispering about her. For the first time in her life Rosa felt very much alone. What could she do? If she booked into this hotel she had no money to pay her bills. She could live on credit for a while, but if she was leaving Mike she did not want him to have to provide for her. She had no skills to secure work. No, she would have to admit defeat. She would go home.

'So, you're back.' Don Emilio looked up from his desk when she lightly knocked and entered his study. 'Well, I am not one to say I told you so.'

'You forced me to marry him. It was foolish of me to give you cause. I am beginning to think it might all have been a big mistake.'

'So, you have come to your senses? You see him now for what he is, a hothead, a chancer, a man of alley-cat morals — '

'No, I don't see him that way at all. I still love him. But I want to think things over. I'm not sure what I shall do. I just want to rest.'

Don Emilio came from around his desk and hugged her to him with one arm. 'It's all over. I'm glad you are back. I will get in touch with my lawyer and arrange a legal separation.'

'No,' she cried. 'Don't do that. Not yet.'

He studied her, her finely chiselled face, the translucently pale skin other women envied so. 'You are sunburned,' he said. 'Your arms so scratched. You smell of camp-fires. That is not the life for you.'

'Father, I've been wondering, would it be possible for me to open an orphanage, or a free hospital for the poor in the town? I would like to do some good with my life.'

'For goodness sake!' He released her and returned to his desk. 'What good is a hospital for these ignorant *peons*.

They would rather have the *curandera* prescribe some magic potion.'

'But infant mortality, it is terrible. Surely we could do something to help.'

'Forget such absurd ideas, Rosa. The *peons* pop out babies like a pile of beans. What would happen if they all lived to your grandmother's age? Mexico would be swamped with people. God has his ways of controlling the population.'

'God and the church!' Rosa felt the old anger and irritation with her father returning. 'That is not the answer. He is a great solace for sorrow, I know. But I am not blind and deaf. Everywhere there is talk of change. Don Porfirio cannot stay on top of his pinnacle for ever. His position, our position, is very wobbly. One day we may all come toppling down.'

'Quiet!' her father commanded. 'As soon as you are back here you start spouting like some rabid revolutionary. I have given my allegiance to the president and I for one will never abandon him.'

'Open your eyes, Father. Isn't it time we put our house in order? Or do you want to suffer the same fate as Grandfather?'

'Put my house in order? I look after my *vaqueros* from the cradle to the grave.'

'You could pay them a wage.'

'A wage? What rubbish. You don't know those men. They would only drink it, woman it, or gamble it away. They get their keep, their allowance of wine. What more can they need?'

'What about your slaves?'

Don Emilio had picked up his quill and turned to his accounts. 'Slaves?'

'Yes, the Yaqui Indians who work in your mine. If you look back in that book you will see you paid twenty-five pesos each for them. They were brought here in chains ten years ago. They are still slaves.'

'They are prisoners of war. They were attacking our villages in the north. What would you prefer me to do — hang them all?' He reached out and tugged at

176

a bell-pull. 'This conversation is over. I don't want to hear its like again.'

Rosa stood in silence, biting her lip, beginning to wish she had not returned here.

'I understand that that madman, your husband, is skimping on the foundations of his bridge,' Don Emilio remarked. 'Soon he will be finished, too. He will have to quit.'

'I might be a quitter,' Rosa responded, fierily. 'But I can assure you Mike Morgan will never quit. He'd rather die first.'

When a maid appeared, Don Emilio called, 'Can you take Rosa to her room? She will be needing a hot tub and fresh clothes laid out. Go now, dear. I will see you at dinner tonight.'

★ ★ ★

Morgan was being shaken awake. He opened his eyes wondering what he was doing amid a pile of boulders on a steep ravine-side and saw Rowdy's bearded face. 'What's happened?'

But it was all coming back to him as he reached a hand to his pounding head and saw his palm covered with blood. 'Where's the engine?'

'At the foot of the crik with the flatbed and crane. But the bridge is still in one piece apart from a few struts at this end. You're lucky to be alive. Can you move?'

'Yeah, I think so.' Mike groaned as he tried to get up. 'Give us a hand.'

'Take it easy. You got a nasty crack to your cranium.'

Mike leaned on his shoulder to steady himself and stretched. 'Seem to be OK. Nothing broken. How's the engineer?'

'Dead. Crushed under the engine.'

Morgan did not reply, staring down dazedly at the big locomotive which, belly-up, appeared to be lodged against the bridge's foundations.

'Waal, that would appear to be the end of this railroad. I'd better git you back up to the top, ol' pal.'

'It ain't the end,' Morgan growled

when he stood at the top of the precipice among the Chinese and *peons* who crowded around. 'I ain't finished yet.'

'Murphy and his two Irish colleagues have been murdered,' Rowdy said. 'Face the facts, Mike, they've won. This project was jinxed from the start.'

'This is war,' Morgan gritted out. 'My war. And I'll say when it's finished.'

Suddenly a ripple of excitement ran through the labourers which turned to cheering as they spotted another locomotive shooting smoke up into the air, its rods churning as it laboured up the track.

'It's Pop,' Rowdy shouted. 'Durn me! He's got that cargo of rails with him. He musta collected them in Puerto and commandeered the passenger engine.'

Pop was blasting his steam whistle as he came along around the side of the mountain. 'I knew my pal in Arizona wouldn't let me down,' he shouted, as he eased to a halt at the end of the line of trucks. 'I got a present all the way from California.'

'Bless you.' Mike hugged him, picked off his hat and planted a kiss on his bald head. 'You're a miracle-worker.'

'Hey, what's happened to you?' Pop hollered, looking at his torn, dusty, bloodstained clothes. 'You look like you been run over by a stampede.'

'Bloody but unbowed.' Mike grinned. 'It's a long, sad story. Tell him, Rowdy. I gotta git these rails unloaded and start the men laying track. Then I'm taking the locomotive back to Santa Rosa.'

Both men stared at him, uneasily. 'What you going there for?' Rowdy asked.

'I got unfinished business,' Morgan growled.

11

Luke Jones spun the cylinder of his shiny, nickel-plated Sidewinder as he sprawled on a rattan chair in the bar of the Hotel Real. 'Waal, that settled Morgan's hash,' he drawled. 'They won't be goin' nowhere.'

'Yuh.' Hank Pike took a slug of tequila. 'Hear tell the California and Gulch gang are goin' ahead by leaps and bounds, heading along the side of the volcano. There's no stopping us gettin' to the mine first now.'

'What'n hell're you chawin' on that stuff fer, Luke?' Baker growled. 'What is it?'

Jones tore another lump from the grey sheet he had bought in the marketplace. 'Chewing gum,' he grinned. 'From the chewing-gum-tree. Thought I'd give it a try.' He spat out a used lump and stuck the other piece inside his cheek.

'Cain't say it's got much taste.'

'But what's the point of it?' Baker pressed.

'Dunno.' Luke chewed rhythmically. 'There's some fella in the States is buying it up, flavouring it with peppermint and selling li'l packets of it. He's making a fortune.'

'Don't be stupid,' Hank shouted. 'Who the hell's gonna stand around looking like a cow chawin' cud all day? Only a moron.'

'The Mexicans seem to like it.'

'They'd like anything. You seen the stuff they eat? Fried locusts, bits of pig-skin. Come on.' He got to his feet, hitching up the long-barrelled Remington revolver on his lanky thigh. 'Let's celebrate 'fore we go back and claim our cash from Al. Hey,' he called to the bartender. 'Where's the best whorehouse around here?'

'Looks more like a warehouse,' Luke remarked when they found the place along a cobbled lane. He kicked open a door. 'After me, boys.'

The shady bodega was stacked with barrels in the loft and lined up each side of the cellar. A makeshift bar was down one end, planks balanced on a couple more barrels. The surly-looking owner got up from his barrel chair to greet them. '*¿Sí, qué pasa?*'

'Where's the gals?' Luke crooned, spurs jangling as he hip-swung in his *vaquero* outfit. 'Or we in the wrong place?'

The *propietario* scratched at his unshaven jaw and yawned. 'You got the cash to pay? Fine girls don't come cheap.'

'Sure, we're loaded.' Luke clattered a handful of silver pesos on to the plank bar. 'Bring 'em on. What you got to drink?'

'What's in the barrels. Wine, sherry, pulque, tequila. What you want?' He turned the spigot of a barrel and drew off a tumbler of red. 'Try that. The best.'

'Nah, I'll stick to tequila. How about you, Hank? Pulque for George, I know.'

'Sure, I'm partial to a drop of dago red now 'n' again,' Pike said, sniffing the tumblerful like a connoisseur.

'Juanita!' the *propietario* hollered. 'Teresa! Get out here. You got customers.'

'Jeez!' Luke squawked, as the two young women stumbled out from behind a curtained-off partition. 'What's this? One's skinny as a rake. T'other's fat as a hog. Where's t'others?'

'Take them or leave them,' their pimp replied in Spanish. 'They are all I have. Very nice girls. Very clean. Ready to please your every whim.'

'This un'll do me,' Pike snarled, grabbing hold of the skinny one by her black hair. 'Where's the crib?'

Teresa squealed with pain as the tall *hombre* dragged her towards the curtain, losing her temper, trying to fight him off. Pike cracked her across the jaw with his open hand, making her head spin. 'Yeah, fight me, you wildcat. That's the way I like it.'

'Hey,' the *propietario* roared. 'Less of the rough stuff. There's no need for that.'

'What you gonna do about it, brother?' Pike hung on to Teresa's hair and patted his sixgun.

The *propietario* frowned, shrugged, then concentrated on filling a clay *olla* with pulque for Baker.

'This un's big enough fer both of us.' Luke hugged the Indian woman's buxom bosoms to him as she giggled in embarrassment. 'Hey, darlin', try some tequila.'

★   ★   ★

Morgan had helped the coolies manhandle the heavy rails and spikes from the cars. 'Come on,' he shouted. 'I'm in a hurry.'

There was an ominous rumble of thunder as black clouds billowed up behind the volcano. 'It don't look good,' Rowdy said. 'What'll we do about all these stiffs: Murphy and co, and Jock the engineer?'

Morgan swung up into the cab of the locomotive, with one of the Chinese to act as fireman. 'Bury 'em,' he shouted. 'What else can you do?'

In the climb from Santa Rosa the engine had built up a good head of steam, so it was ready to move back out. Mike was familiar with the general principles of the steam-engine, that the water in the boiler was heated by hot-air tubes from the firebox, and steam was generated as boiling water collected in the dome, but he was momentarily flummoxed by the array of wheels and handles. 'How do I get it in reverse?' he yelled.

Pop climbed up to demonstrate. 'You gotta watch the dial of the pressure gauge,' he explained, testing the handle. 'Make sure the needle's swung to high. See? You're on your way.'

He released the brake and fed steam into the cylinders controlled by the slide valve. The pistons began to move backwards and forwards as the connect-ing rods' crank started turning the wheels. 'Up is reverse, down is forward. Simple, ain't it? So long, my friend, it's all yours.' Pop backed out of the cab to step off and shouted, 'You oughta do something about that cut to your head.'

Yes, it was easy enough once you got the hang of it; in fact there was a fine feeling of power as the stack churned out woodsmoke, and the locomotive pushed the empty vans before it rattling down the track. Soon they were eating up the miles as his scrawny fireman fed in more logs.

'They ain't gittin' away with it this time,' Morgan gritted out.

Big blobs of rain had begun to splash slowly into the dust as he eased the locomotive into Santa Rosa, but the rumbling storm had yet to break. Morgan wondered despondently whether he was going to be proved wrong, if all this work and effort, death, blood, sweat, tears, had all been in vain.

But he had no time to lose. He grabbed his Winchester — he had lost his Smith & Wesson in the explosion — and, in his torn clothes, blood encrusting his tangled hair, he limped down the street to the paved plaza, the Hotel Real.

'You seen any sign of that tall *hombre*, Hank Pike?' he demanded of the bartender. 'An' two other bozos'?'

He repeated the question in Spanish and the barkeep cried, 'Ah, *sí*, Hank and his *amigos*. They have gone to the bordello. The same one I sent you to.'

'Right.' Morgan drew himself up and checked the Winchester, then headed out of the hotel. As he neared the bodega he licked his lips, nervously. Well, anybody would feel tense in a situation like this. All three were professional fast guns. They would have no hesitation in killing. He needed to get the drop on them. But how? Maybe if he nosed around the back . . . ?

* * *

'Makes a change to meet a real man, eh, baby?' Pike grinned broken teeth at Teresa as she lay sprawled on the dirty mattress, her face bruised, her dress torn. He buttoned up and flicked a five-peso piece at her derisively. 'That's the going price, ain't it?'

He wandered back out into the cellar. 'Ain't you two done yet? Come on, we gotta git outa here.'

'Hang on,' Luke squawked. He had the Indian woman down on her knees. 'This fat piggy takes some seein' to.'

George was sat on a barrel quaffing his cloudy liquor. 'Go on,' he growled, 'give it to her.'

Suddenly barrels crashed down from the loft to skittle George Baker off his seat, his *olla* of Mexican beer smashing as he hit the flags. 'Where 'n hell did you come from?' he shouted, fumbling to pull his Colt .45, staring up at the shadowy figure in the loft.

'I've come for vengeance.'

Morgan had climbed on to a high cart at the back of the building and crawled through a cobwebbed window into the loft. For moments he had watched the men roistering. He was reluctant to shoot even a backshooter in the back.

'This is for Murphy, his two men, my engineer, Jock, Wang, Jorge . . . all the others.'

As Baker pulled his Colt he blasted him off his feet. The desperado subsided into a pool of blood.

'Jesus!' Luke rolled over on to his back, hanging on to Juanita, keeping her on top of him, a fat female shield, as he slid out his Sidewinder and pumped lead at Morgan. 'Die!'

The naked Indian woman howled, kicking her legs and waving her arms like a beetle struggling to get back on its feet. With a titanic effort she succeeded and scrambled away as Morgan kicked another barrel tumbling down.

Luke Jones, exposed, had no alternative but to try to fend off the barrel and stand to face the Texan, fanning out his last slugs. Morgan levered the Winchester and his shot hit Luke full in the chest, blasting through his heart. As he crumpled to the floor Jones groaned, 'How do you kill this guy?'

'Like this!' Pike shouted above the din of the explosions, aiming up through the floorboards. One of the powerful Remington's .44s scorched up Morgan's thigh making him leap aside like a scalded cat as more slugs smashed through the boards.

'Jeez!' he whistled. 'You nearly ruined my marital prospects.' He levered the carbine again and fired back down through the splintered loft floor. 'Two can play at that game.'

'No!' the *propietario* begged. 'No more!' He made a dash for the door, shrieking, 'Call the *rurales*!'

The shot floorboards suddenly creaked and collapsed, pitching Morgan through. He landed badly, twisting his leg on the plank bar as he hit the floor, the Winchester knocked flying from his grasp.

'Gotcha!' Pike crowed, aiming the Remington, arm outstretched, as Morgan knelt helplessly before him. 'This is the last time you interfere.'

Pike was about to pull the trigger when his face grimaced with pain. A sharp knife had thudded from behind into his already injured shoulder. He spun around and saw Teresa beside the drawn curtain, her hand raised from the throw. 'You bitch!'

The Remington crashed out and the girl was sent spinning. Morgan tried to save her, making a scissor kick at the gunman's legs, bringing him down, but he was too late.

He retrieved the Winchester as Pike scrambled away, turning at the door to fire again. Morgan levered the carbine but the magazine was empty. Luckily for him Pike didn't know that and slipped out of the open door. When he reached the street Hank was running away as fast as his boots would carry him. He reached a corner and was gone from sight.

'Damn him!' Morgan said, dismayed. 'He's got away again.'

When he returned to kneel beside

Teresa she was dying fast, blood pumping from the inch-hole between her breasts. 'Please,' she whispered. 'My child. What will happen to him?'

Morgan heard a baby's cry coming from a back room. 'He'll be OK,' he said, holding her hand. 'I owe you. You don't deserve this.'

* * *

Don Emilio had persuaded his daughter to ride in his coach with him that morning to let the towns-people see that he and Rosa were as close as ever and to silence any sneers and gossip about her marriage. He handed her into the Hotel Real and they took their seats in the foyer beneath the new portrait of the great benefactor, President Diaz, with his magnificent eagle-winged moustache.

'He would hardly have room for any more medals on his chest.' Rosa smiled impishly. 'Perhaps he has some pinned on his backside.'

'Quiet,' her father hissed. 'You could be thrown into jail for such impertinence. What has come over you?'

He glared at her as angrily as Diaz, ordered French brandy, and brushed raindrops from his hair. 'Soon the deluge will commence,' he said, referring to the tropical rains that would cascade down for a month or more. 'Then we will see how clever your husband is. Will his bridge hold? I doubt it.'

Rosa did not reply for she, too, had her doubts. Mike was unaware of how hard the rain came down in these parts. She savoured a cool lime-juice cordial and wondered where he was, why he had not come to look for her. It was good to feel clean, civilized again, she had to admit. Her starched underskirts rustled beneath a ruffled, green-silk dress, above her fine black stockings and high-heeled shoes. She, too, tossed back her hair and flicked rain from her head, from her black velvet bolero. Was it a sin to enjoy feeling feminine?

She was not too pleased to see Ferdinand Lopez, flashily attired as always, enter the hotel, join them and help himself to brandy from the bottle.

'How's Mike?' she replied, in answer to his query. 'He's very well, as far as I know.'

'Good.' Lopez grinned, and rasped out, 'Musta been misinformed. Heard he mighta had an accident.'

'What?' she exclaimed, and her heart banged even more in her chest as she saw her husband climbing the steps to the hotel.

'What was that shooting just now?' Don Emilio was demanding, and then Mike Morgan was standing before them, swaying on his feet, shirt and trousers torn, muddy and bloodstained. 'Oh, I might have known. Wherever you go there's trouble.'

'I jest been cleanin' out a nest of rats,' Morgan drawled. 'Mr King Rat's skedaddled. Hank Pike. You ain't seen him by any chance?'

'Mike!' Rosa saw the gash, the

congealed blood in his damp, tousled hair and got to her feet. 'What's happened to you?'

'Stay where you are, Rosa. There might well be more trouble if there's any more rats around.' He glowered at Lopez. 'Like this one, fer instance. Now, here's a real snake in the grass.'

'What you talking about, gringo?' Ferdinand blustered in his guttural manner. 'Everybody knows you're crazy. You better go lie down a bit.'

Morgan had abandoned the Winchester for he had forgotten, in his haste, to bring any more ammunition. He had limped on his twisted leg through the lanes looking for Pike but he seemed to have high-tailed it.

'So, it ain't true that you're in cahoots with the California Gulf boys, that you pocketed cash to divert our cargo of rails down to them?'

Don Emilio looked appalled. 'Is that true, Ferdinand?'

'I wouldn't be surprised if he had plenty to do with all the rest, the attacks on us, the murders, our engine being dynamited into the ravine.' Lopez did not appear to be armed so Morgan shouted, 'Come outside, you leech. I'm gonna beat you to pulp.'

'Calm down.' Lopez flashed his teeth in apparent puzzlement, reaching inside his suit as he sat there as if for a cigarette. He brought out the Mauser automatic. 'You got too big a mouth. This'll shut it.'

'No!' Don Emilio had jumped forward to restrain him. 'Ah,' he sighed, crumpling forward as two slugs pumped into him, 'you fool, Ferdinand . . . '

Lopez hurled him aside, jumped to his feet and aimed the Mauser at Morgan. It spat lead as he leaped aside, jerking out Luke's Sidewinder, which he had tucked into the back of his waistband, and giving the Mexican the full flavour of its .38s.

Both men continued firing until their bullets were spent and, as the acrid gunsmoke wafted around them, it was Ferdinand who bared his teeth in a final rictus grin and toppled to the floor.

Morgan poked him warily with his boot, but he was dead. Rosa was on her knees beside her father, patting his hand, trying to bring him round. The colour was fast draining from his cheeks. He looked up at Morgan and croaked out, 'I was wrong to make you marry my daughter. But what's done's done. Please, my last request, be good to her.'

The Texan knelt beside her and gripped the older man's hand. 'We never did much see eye to eye, you an' me,' he said. 'But that's a deal.'

12

'I gotta get back to the bridge,' Morgan shouted as the rain flattened his hair across his brow. 'You see to your father. I'll be back.'

'Mike!' Rosa screamed, but he was already limping away across the plaza and a crack of thunderous lightning tore the heavens apart, drowning her voice.

Suddenly it occurred to her: what is the hurry now to get to the mine? The death of her father made his contract with them null and void. But she knew it was just stubborn pride. Getting the railroad to the mine was all that mattered to Mike Morgan. And, anyway, she had too many other matters on her mind as the jefe of *rurales* came running up, demanding to know what was going on. She would have to try to explain. And there was her grandmother to break the news to, as well.

The Chinese fireman had done well, keeping the boiler primed, and he was ready to move out as Morgan joined him on the footplate. The Texan looked apprehensively at the black boiling clouds moving towards them from the mountains and gritted out, 'C'mon, let's go.'

The storm suddenly hit the workers at the bridge with all its intensity, rods of rain cascading down. Pop had foreseen what might happen and had ordered the *peons* and coolies to roll rocks down to the foot of the narrow ravine to shore up the engine and flatbed crane against the sides of the bridge's foundations.

He blew a whistle shrilly and beckoned to them to get out. 'Come on,' he shouted. 'There's nothing more we can do. It's too late now.'

When he reached the top he heard the whoo-whooing of the locomotive's steam siren and saw the engine, with its tall stack blowing smoke, and its cowcatcher in front, charging back up the track.

'All we can do now is keep our fingers crossed,' Pop shouted as Morgan jumped from the footplate and joined them beside the bridge. 'We've done our best to patch it up.'

The colossal tropical cloudburst was far worse than any of them had anticipated. When it hit the crests of the mountains the water ran off down their steep sides in innumerable rivulets and streams, feeding each other, getting higher, wider, deeper until there was one wild, raging wall of water some forty feet high, taking everything with it: shrubs, fallen tree trunks, debris, as it cascaded down.

'Holy jeepers!' Pop cried with awe when he saw it coming. 'Hang onto your hats, boys. Here it comes!'

They stared, speechless, as the turbulent wall of water, like some avenging Niagara, rushed towards the bridge. Suddenly it hit. The whole structure shook and groaned. But it withstood the shock as the river poured through. They stood a long while watching until Morgan shouted, triumphantly, 'It's gonna hold!'

Rowdy and Pop were dancing around with each other in the mud and rain as Morgan drawled, 'They did us a good turn blowing up the engine. That's what's holding it firm.'

★ ★ ★

The California & Gulf did not have the same luck. The placid Rio Tinto suddenly became a monster, raging and swelling, bursting its banks. All along the line the railroad and its foundations were swamped and broken, much of it swept away down to the estuary.

When Hank Pike reached the construction camp office he found Al Stevens in despair, sitting at his desk, his head in his hands. 'I'm ruined,' he moaned, hitting the whiskey hard. 'This'll finish me with the company.'

'In that case,' Pike snarled, levelling his Remington at him, 'you won't be needing what you got in your safe. Hand over the keys.'

'You're crazy,' Al pleaded.

'Yeah, maybe I am.' The revolver blasted out lead and Al was removed from his seat. He hit the wall and stared dazedly as he succumbed.

Hank found his keys and his wallet, opened the big safe. 'Hey, hey,' he gloated, as he saw the stack of greenbacks and pesos. 'It's pay-day for me, if not the boys. This storm's brought me good luck.'

He unceremoniously pulled off Al's trousers, knotted string around the bottoms and stuffed the notes and silver into them, pulling the belt tight. Outside, he slung his loot over the neck of his mustang, glanced up at the sky, climbed into the saddle and set off, plodding away along the river in the falling rain. He planned to escape through the mountains and head for San Luis Potosi where they had been mining silver since 1703. There might be even richer pickings for him before he returned to the States.

★ ★ ★

Hank Pike was crouched over his camp-fire some days later, roasting a rattlesnake for his supper. He had stolen it from a chaparral cock after watching, fascinated, as it fought its prey. Then he deprived the victor of his spoils.

'This is gonna be real tasty,' he chuckled, but froze as some sixth sense warned him that he was not alone. He slid his fingers towards his Remington but only had it half-out when a rifle barrel poked him in the back.

'Hey, gringo, you better not do that or I will be forced to blow you to kingdom come.'

Suddenly he was surrounded by Mexicans, cackling with glee at their catch, whooping even more when they slit Al's stuffed pants and notes and silver showered out.

They were a scurvy band, draped with bandoliers of bullets, attired in ragged leathers to protect them as they rode through the chaparral, sporting enormous sombreros. 'Have a heart, boys,' Pike pleaded. 'You may be bandits, but I am, too. I could be of use to you. Why don't I jine ya?'

'We are not *bandidos*,' their chief declared. 'We are revolutionaries. Soon we will take over Mexico. Diaz will be put before a firing-squad. So will all the *haciendados* and thieving *Americanos*.'

He turned to his men and shouted, 'What shall we do with him! Shall we cut off his ears and the soles of his feet and use him for target practice?'

'No, *jefe*,' one cried, grinning evilly as he took a pot of honey from his saddle-bag. 'Let's make it a slower, more painful death for this one.'

They stripped Pike naked and, laughingly, teased him as they spread honey over his body, face and hair, then pegged him to the ground close to an antheap.

'Look,' one laughed, 'they have got scent of him.'

Pike craned his head, saw the line of ants approaching, hungrily alert. Soon they would be crawling busily over him, nibbling away at this unexpected treat.

'Aw, shee-it!' Pike groaned. 'What a way to go.'

★　★　★

A lot had happened in six weeks. Rosa's grandmother had fast followed Don Emilio to the grave, her death probably brought on by the shock of it all. Rosa had found herself the sole inheritor of vast lands and wealth. It took some while to get used to this idea, but she knew what she wanted to do. She would turn the town house into an orphanage and free school. She would give the mine and railroad to Pop to run, on condition that he released the Yaqui slaves from their shackles, allowed them to return to their homeland, and paid the other *peons* a living wage. 'You and

Rowdy know about cattle,' she told Morgan. 'I wan' you to have the hacienda and *rancho*.'

'I don't want your money,' he growled. 'I didn't marry you for that.'

'But you have married me so now what's mine is yours. In Mexico the woman has few rights. It is up to her husband to decide what is done. And while we're talking about that,' she smiled, 'I want a proper church wedding.'

The whole town turned out for their second nuptials to cheer them, and wish them well, maybe because Rosa had donated a steer to be roasted on the plaza, and barrels of wine for consumption. It had been quite a feast.

'What are we gonna do about Teresa's baby boy?' he asked after the service.

'He will be a brother to our new one.' She patted a slight bulge in her abdomen. 'I didn't want to tell you until I was sure.'

'Hey,' he yelled, kissing her, 'I musta

done somethang right that first night after all!'

That night as they lay together she whispered to him, 'My only fear is what will happen to us when the revolution comes, for it surely will. It was terrible the last time, so many *haciendados* killed, their lands and titles confiscated, priests and nuns persecuted, the churches looted.'

'We'll cross that bridge when we come to it,' he said. 'But what with you doin' all these missionary works and me punchin' cows, they might go easy on us. If it don't work out we can allus go an' live in Texas.'

★ ★ ★

In mid-October the rains were coming to an end, but great clouds still cast their shadows racing across the plains. Rosa on her white stallion, and Morgan on a mustang, were riding across the high plateau towards the mine to see how Pop was getting on. The ground was spangled with flowers, multi-coloured cosmos and brilliant blue lupins, and picturesque with ancient fumaroles. Before them soared the volcano, its snowy cap seeming to hover amid its cloud. The Plumed Serpent, the Indians called it, but this particular serpent hadn't spat out its plume of burning lava since 1803. Often, however, it would mumble threateningly, coughing up sulphurous embers, and the *peons* would turn their heads to it with awe.

'Come on,' Rosa cried. 'It's not far now. I'll give you a race.' They were now only a mile or so from the mine and could see it in the distance.

There was no catching her as she sent Blaze haring away, but eventually she reined in and they were laughingly reunited. They stepped down for a breather, to water the horses, and rest beside a clear stream. They were in no hurry.

'Sometimes,' it occurred to him, 'I wonder what happened to that fella

Pike. He's probably back in Missouri counting all that cash he stole.'

'He will roast in hell,' Rosa said, lying back in the grass to breathe in the clear mountain air, watch a pair of eagles circling in the blue sky. 'Why worry about him, Mike?' she smiled, drawing him to her. 'There are so many better things to do.'

THE END